The
One
&
Only

ISBN-13: 978-0-9950979-7-1

ALSO BY MARIA LA SERRA

The Proverbial Mr.Universe

Lyrical Lights

Pour toi chère maman

" After a terrible breakup, there's no amount of therapy that can make you feel brand-new like a pair of stilettos. Never underestimate their power, they make you believe you can conquer the world. "

8 Ways to Get Over a Breakup
by Staci Cortés

1

STACI

"MEN ARE LIKE SHOES," my *abuela* had once said, feeling compelled to share some of her wisdom. "Take all things into account before committing. What is it going to cost you? Do they go with everything in your wardrobe? But the most important thing is comfort. If you keep buying shoes too tight, where will that leave you? With bunions— so choose wisely."

Ultimately, my whole adult life, I'd been wearing shoes one size smaller, but what my intrusive grandmother hadn't understood was singlehood suited me fine. I was at a place in my life where things were great. Why should I compromise that for any man? I'd earned those bunions—it'd strengthened me.

Rushing into the lobby of the ornate limestone building, I'd feared I might be late this morning, but I couldn't pass up the shoe sale at Barneys. So I didn't have a guy in my life, but at least I had Christian Louboutin. He was the only man worth making space for in my closet. I was lucky that my salary supported my shoe fetish. At twenty-six years old, I had been a dating columnist for *Starlet* magazine for the last two years. Ironic, here I was, single and giving other women advice about how to snag the right guy, but I was better at giving advice than following my own. With a journalism degree, my goal was to one day work for the *New York Times*. If only I could get my foot in the door somehow and build my portfolio to show off my writing prowess. In the meantime, I can't complain as I was still working for a reputable company. *Starlet* was a division of Nast Publishing, a large mass media company based in New York. That could give me connections to a plethora of job opportunities if I wanted them—that was, if I made a name for myself.

My heels clicked as I walked through the high-ceiling lobby with my Prada purse over my shoulder. I pushed the button for the elevator, and it instantly dinged open. My stomach turned when I saw the face of the man staring at me.

"Going up?" Greg McAdams asked, holding the elevator door open. "I literally just got in here. No wonder it hasn't gone up yet."

I looked down my nose at him as I entered the elevator, flipping the thick locks of my black hair in his face before pushing number twelve. Then I backed into the corner, resting against the railing as I glared at him. "Shouldn't you be on vacation or something?" I snapped.

"Got back yesterday," he said, putting his hands into the pockets of his dress pants.

I had to admit, he had a good sense of style in his tailored blue suit paired with a matching tie, but I'd be damned if I ever told him. That smug twenty-nine-year-old flashed a pearly white smile, looking at me with his deep blue eyes. His brown light hair was slicked back with too much product, and he looked like he hadn't shaved in a few days, yet his facial hair still looked tidy.

He makes me sick— why did he have to be my type?

"Can I help you with something?" he asked in his smooth, deep voice.

"No," I said, jerking my gaze away from him as I crossed my arms.

We stood there in silence until we had to get off on the same floor. Greg worked in the office across the hall from mine at *Avant-Garde*, also a division of Nast, doing the same job as me but for male readers. He had the second-biggest office on the floor, but I guessed it was nice when your father owned the company. I, on the other hand, worked hard to get where I was.

I could tell by the sharp look in his eyes he thought he was better than me. Most men who drove a silver 1967 Ferrari 365 Spyder on the verge of being thirty had that aura, like a pre-midlife crisis. He was a playboy in every sense of the word.

When the elevator door opened, I shoved my way past Greg. But before I turned the corner, I looked over my shoulder with a mischievous smile. I assumed he was staring at my tight backside, as most men did when I walked away. I wanted him to stare to see what he could never have. It was probably the greatest revenge I could get without trying.

The central office hub was packed with desks of assistants, writers, and editors with one closed-off office in the corner for the editor-in-chief. As I passed the rows of cubicles making my way to my desk, the phones were ringing off the hook. The staff slowly answered them, some after a giant swig of coffee. As for me, I drank tea. My body was a sanctuary, and I couldn't put that kind of caffeine into it.

Plopping into my desk chair, I turned on my computer. As I sat there waiting for my laptop to load up, I felt like someone was watching me. My desk neighbor, Jackie, was peering at me with a huge smile on her adorable face.

"Good morning," I said as she broke into a smile. "What is it? You look like you want to say something."

Jackie struggled to hold back a squeal while she pushed up

her cute glasses with little hearts on them that she used for reading.

She rolled her chair toward me. "You won't believe what I heard about you," she whispered, leaning closer.

"Me?" I leaned in, too, wondering what secret we were about to share.

"The phones never ring this much unless one of our writers publishes a huge story and needs to be interviewed, right?" she asked.

"That happens, like, once in a blue moon." I chuckled. "We do makeup tips and celebrity gossip, but there's never anything substantial, except that one time when Julia discovered which young celebrity had an eating disorder. That was a moving piece."

"Forget about Julia," she said, bouncing in her seat. "Your article—'Why the Millennial Woman Should Vote'—is now live online!"

"What? I thought Kate was pulling the plug on the assignment."

Kate was my boss. The last time we'd spoken, it was about where I saw my career progressing at *Starlet*. I wanted to write more about things that mattered to me, like what was going on in the world besides how to find the perfect man, but Kate had said the magazine wasn't ready to go there yet. I'd thought maybe they never would. But now?

"You should be proud of yourself. *Starlet* has been getting amazing feedback on their website comment section. The public loves you!"

My jaw dropped as I lunged forward to hug Jackie. "Oh, that's such great news! So, what does that mean? Am I being interviewed? Photo shoot? Getting some woman's award? What?" I giggled because I knew, as long as I wrote under *Starlet*'s banner, no one would take my work seriously.

Jackie's smile faded, as she twiddled her thumbs. "Well ... if you're going to say it like that, my news seems pointless now."

"Oh, don't be like that," I said, chewing on the end of my pen. A huge smile crossed my face, and I hugged Jackie again. "I'm so glad you told me because it means a lot. I know I sometimes complain about not being able to write more political pieces, but moments like this are exceptional." I logged into the company's website to read the glowing comments, ignoring the negative ones. I was ecstatic—nothing would bring my mood down.

"Well, I know this isn't your dream job. You might be saying that for the boss's benefit." Jackie's eyelids drooped.

I waved my hand in dismissal. "You should know me by now. I say nothing I don't mean—I don't care who hears it," I said. "Besides, the only reason I haven't left *Starlet* is because I'd miss working with you."

"Do you mean that?"

"Of course," I said.

I enjoyed working with Jackie. She was our beauty editor. She'd been covering skincare, makeup, and hair for the last five years at *Starlet*.

"Do you want to go out tonight to celebrate? Dinner maybe? Or just drinks if you have to tend to your family first."

Jackie rolled back to her desk, picking up where she left off writing one of her makeup articles. "My kids know how hard I work. I could use a night out at a bar. I just have to call my husband."

She fluffed her curly brown hair before pulling her cell phone out of her purse. I studied her slim build and gorgeous gray pantsuit, wondering if she'd always been that thin and beautiful. At thirty-nine, she had two kids and job security for life. She always joked about how she'd get replaced by a younger model, but her column was so popular that Kate, our editor-in-chief, would be an idiot to ever get rid of her.

As I listened to her talk on the phone to her husband, saying, "I love you" several times before making smooching noises, I was a little jealous of her high-school-sweetheart romance. I was glad she was with such a loving man, as she deserved to be happy.

I'd only had two serious boyfriends in my life—one back in college, but that wasn't true love, and Luis, who I had been with for two good years until, one day, his mother showed up at my doorstep.

She'd hugged me while crying, "I can't believe Luis broke up with you!"

There I was standing, baffled, wearing a fresh yogurt facial mask and flannel pajamas, consoling Luis's mother about our breakup I had known nothing about. I had no clue this was coming. I thought things with Luis were great. He made me believe we would have a future together. That, at some point, we would get married and buy a fixer-upper somewhere in Brooklyn, remodelling it to look modern chic. We would adopt a dog, a cocker spaniel or two, like Oprah. I even dedicated a whole board on Pinterest labeled Luis and Staci's Wedding Ideas. I had our lives planned out. Then, the night before his trip to San Diego, Luis told me how much he loved me—how he hated being apart, but then he got his mother to break up with me.

What kind of person did that? Lie about loving someone?

He was an emotional masochist and I'd somehow missed all the clues. For one, we'd lived in separate apartments. He never wanted me to spend the night over at his fancy apartment because he needed his space. If I stayed overnight, then I would be inclined to do it again. I never made a big deal about it because he was never home anyway. Luis worked all those shifts at the hospital. But, really, I had been in a relationship with an emotionally-detached man. That alone should have been a red flag.

Anyhow, that was all in the past. It'd been two years now, and with proper therapy and a closet full of Christian Louboutin shoes, I had grown stronger from it. Who needed Mr. Right? I didn't know if I ever wanted to find him in the first place, as my career had been my focus ever since I was nine. Who'd have guessed I would become a relationship columnist because I was just as lost as the next girl. Fake it until you make it ... whatever that meant.

At the end of the day, Jackie and I packed up our things and headed to Polly's for drinks, a bar located a few blocks away. I loved walking there, even with the challenge of heels but by the time we arrived, my feet were killing me and I was eager to get a booth. We entered the dimly-lit bar bustling with clinking glasses and endless chatter from people who just got off work.

Sitting in the cushioned booth across from each other, I ordered us wine and nachos.

Jackie looked at me with wide eyes. "Are you serious?" she asked. "Doesn't that go against your diet? Are you falling off the wagon?"

"I'm not falling off anything." I laughed, shutting the plastic-covered menu. "I like to have a treat every so often. There's nothing wrong with that. Six years of going to the gym every day aren't going to disappear with a few cheesy chips and cabernet," I said.

But I knew I'd come a long way with dealing with my weight. That was why I didn't come out often to these kinds of places. It sometimes caused me anxiety I wouldn't make the right decisions. I realized it wasn't realistic to think I'd gain all eighty-five pounds overnight, but when you'd lost so much, it was hard to see yourself in any other way. It was a constant fear of going back to what you used to look like. I was a size eight, yet when I looked in the mirror, all I saw in the reflection was the size fourteen girl with big hips. It was an everyday struggle, that I never talked about it to anyone, except for Jackie. I knew she was only looking out for me, so I appreciated it, but sometimes she could be overwhelming.

"If you say so." Jackie shrugged, rubbing her hands together when the nachos came.

Steam billowed off the top, and I took a deep whiff of the melted goodness. I was the first to dig in while Jackie savored the aroma.

I spat the chip out onto a plate, fanning my tongue. "They're hot."

"I can see that." Jackie laughed.

For a while, our time out was fun. We gossiped about our coworkers and talked about shopping. Jackie told me about her back-to-school troubles with the kids.

"Now that my oldest is almost a teenager, she's getting really moody. She's so picky about the clothes I buy for her. Can you believe I've had to return half? I guess that's what I get for going alone, but it's always been that way. She hates shopping, and trying to figure out what she wants is a nightmare."

As Jackie continued, I tried to stay focused, but my eyes wandered around the room filled with businessmen and a few attractive women. The front door swung open, allowing the warm breeze to flow inside. It was still light outside, and it wasn't about to get cooler.

"Oh, hell!" I blurted, and Jackie froze mid-sentence.

"What? What's wrong?" she asked, looking up at the door.

"It's Greg," I groaned, choking on his name. "He just walked in. Now, he's about to order the most expensive whiskey on the shelf."

"How do you know?" She laughed.

I peered at her, my eyebrows raised. "I know all about guys like him. The kind that spares no expense or doesn't think about their actions until the consequences arise. He tries to show people he's classy but whatever, he's a fake."

Jackie blew hard on a nacho before popping it in her mouth. She sipped her wine then said with her mouth full, "Are you sure? He seems charming, though I've only seen him a few times in the elevator or at joint company functions."

"Yeah, the functions he's forced to come to since he's the heir of Nast Publishing." I sighed. "Sadly, one day, he will be our boss. I only hope to move on to better horizons when that happens. Take my word for it; he's a dog—not the cute, cuddly kind."

I stared at him, fuming, as he held a beer while chatting with an attractive female bartender. She giggled at his every word, and I knew by the end of her shift, she would go home with Greg. Unfortunately, I stared way too long that Greg saw me and waved. I bowed my head, covering my face with my hand as he headed toward us.

"Crap," I grumbled.

As he approached, Jackie perked up, folded her hands on the table. "Hi, Greg!"

She beamed, and I wanted to throw up.

"What brings you here?" Jackie asked.

I sat up straight, my lips pursed, ignoring his existence while I picked up a nacho.

"I come here sometimes after work," he said. "I had planned to come with a buddy of mine, but he canceled on me at the last minute."

"Ah, that's no fun," Jackie said.

Do not invite him to sit with us, I thought. *Do not invite him to sit with us. Do not—*

"Would you care to join us?" Jackie asked. "We're gossiping and having a few drinks."

Damn it, Jackie!

I cleared my throat, forcing myself to look into Greg's eyes. "I'm sure you have other business to attend to, like hitting on some poor innocent girl you never intend to call back or drink until you black out."

"Well, I wouldn't drink that much on a Tuesday." He chuckled deep in his throat. "But I wouldn't be against getting to bring a beautiful woman back to my apartment. You want to volunteer?" His bright blue eyes danced with mischief.

Jackie laughed. "Oh, Greg. Don't be such a tease."

I stuck my finger in my mouth, pretending to gag. "I'd rather kiss a pig. Oh, wait, you would still qualify then. Never mind."

Greg slid into the seat beside Jackie and she shuffled over closer on my side.

"Don't be so rude," she scolded in her motherly voice. "He was joking. Right, Greg?"

"Of course I'm joking. I like to see Staci all fired up. I'm not her type anyhow," he said to Jackie like I wasn't even there.

"Oh, you've got that right," I said as he flashed me a blank face.

"You are handsome though," Jackie said.

I regurgitated a little in my mouth.

"Thank you," he said, loosening his tie.

He grabbed one of my nachos, and it took everything in me not to slap it out of his hand.

"I rarely listen to what she says," he said, crunching into the chip.

I watched his jaw move up and down, balling my fists. Everything about this man annoyed me.

"I don't like to bring negativity in my life," Greg continued. "It creates bad mojo around me." He made a circling motion with his hands as if he were some spiritual monk.

"Positivity is the way to go," Jackie said, nudging me with her foot under the table.

I blew out a shaky breath. "Fine, I won't say another word," I said, raising my chin.

"Why do you hate me so much?" he said before he took a big gulp of beer.

"You know why," I whispered.

He opened his mouth to speak but then took another sip. Shrugging his shoulders, he slid out of the booth. "I don't want to create any more tension here, so I'll leave you to your ladies' night." With that, he walked off, taking his dark energy with him.

"What is your problem?" Jackie hissed when he was out of earshot. "He was a perfect gentleman, and you blew him off. He's technically a coworker, you know. I've never seen you mistreat anyone before, not even the shoe salesman who forgot to order the correct size for you. Staci, you're a wonderful person, but around him, you're kind of a ..."

"Jerk?" I added flatly.

"That's your word," she blurted. "Why do you hate Greg? You've never told me the whole story. I can see in your eyes something's eating at you."

I finished my wine, slamming the glass on the table. Rising, I slung my purse's strap over my shoulder after dropping cash on the table. "I told you," I mumbled, "Greg plays with women's hearts, and he's the most arrogant man I've ever met. He's a horrible guy, yet everyone seems to love him. I don't get it."

"Is that everything?" she asked, standing beside me, looking over at him.

"Yes," I said after a pause. "The whole story," I lied, but it's the only thing I was ready to disclose.

Linking my arm with hers, I led her out of the bar, bumping Greg's stool on the way. Without looking at her, I knew Jackie had shot me a look to behave. I couldn't help it. Greg brought out a monster in me I couldn't control, not that I wanted to.

66 Women give out signs all the time, and it's important to understand them. If a woman has her arms crossed and her body is leaning away, then she is trying to stop you from getting to know her. Take the hint and back off, especially if she's looking at you like she has daggers in her eyes. Run! You don't want to mess with a woman's fury. 99

How to Decode Nonverbal Signals from Women
by Greg McAdams

2

STACI

"NO, Elena, I'm not letting you sneak a cat into our apartment building. Do you know how much sweet-talking I had to do to get a good deal on our place? If Mr. Arturo finds out I broke the rules, he'll hike up the rent for sure," I said, taking a sip from my coffee mug as I watched her cradle a fluff ball in her arms.

"But I found him on the fire escape. He's so cute," Elena whined. "How can you say no to him?"

"Easy. No. We're not keeping it, and besides, he's too clean to be a stray cat. He probably belongs to someone."

My sister, Elena, was a part-time model studying to be ... I wasn't sure anymore since she kept changing her major.

"There's no tag on his collar," Elena said.

"How do you know it's a *he*?"

"Trust me." She slightly lifted him.

"You should become a veterinarian since you keep bringing these animals home," I said.

"I'll keep that in mind. Are we really going to put him back on the street? It's cold outside."

As she brought the feline closer, I diverted my eyes to our

front door. She knew my weakness. All it took was to look into the cat's big eyes—it did me in.

I sighed. "It's summer. He'll be just fine. If it concerns you that much, just bring him to an animal shelter because I'm not losing this apartment."

We hadn't known when we first rented this place that there was an Italian restaurant located below our apartment with an outdoor seating until two thirty in the morning. At first, I was worried we might have to look for another place. Soon though, I'd discovered the sound of happy laughter coming from outside my window had a positive, curative effect for the aftermath of a broken heart.

"How will Mr. Arturo find out?"

"Mrs. Shaw from across the hall is allergic to cats—that's how."

When I saw the disappointment in her eyes, my stomach took a dip. So I'd lied. I couldn't afford this apartment as it was, and we were three. We had been lucky enough to find another room-mate who was barely around.

I looked down at my watch. "Shoot, I'm running late." I picked up my purse, headed for the door. "Oh, Elena, stop feeding cats on the fire escape!" I shouted before rushing out the door.

I ARRIVED at work just in time to find my nemesis inside the elevator when I rushed to get in. The universe had some sense of humor, repeatedly confining me in tight spaces with Greg McAdams.

"Good morning, Greg," I said through gritted teeth.

After the bar, I'd had a conversation with Jackie, and she'd made me promise to apologize to him.

When I looked at his face, my throat was already closing up. I had to keep my word though even if it killed me, which it might.

"Morning," he said kindly, which pissed me off.

"I'm ..."

He turned, fixing the cuffs of his dress shirt. "Did you say something?"

"I'm sorry," I whispered, looking away from him.

"Come again?"

"I'm sorry!" I huffed, crossing my arms. "Last night, I was rude. I guess you didn't deserve that."

Greg deserved worse, but I had made a promise to Jackie that I would try to behave, at least for today. I looked at him out of the corner of my eye and saw him smiling.

"Wow, who are you? What have you done to my Staci?" he said, walking closer, backing me into the corner. What was that fragrance? That warm, woodsy scent?

Awful.

"That's okay," he said, gazing down at me. "I assumed you were having a bad day. No harm done."

I apologized for nothing, Jackie!

"So," I said, biting my lip. "Did you go home with anyone last night?"

"Actually, I did. The cute bartender practically threw herself at me. We had a wild night. I'll spare your innocence by not going into detail."

"Lucky me," I said with an eye roll.

"What's that?"

"Nothing."

The doors opened, and I pushed Greg out of the way, stomping into the hallway to get to the office. Jackie saw me, giving me a stern expression as she waved me over. I didn't have the opportunity to reach her because Mr. McAdams Senior stepped in front of me.

He wore a brown suit, black loafers, and silver-framed glasses. His eyes were blue with a glimmer of happiness in them that he liked to keep hidden. The hair on his head was grey, disappearing. Then I thought about Greg. In thirty-four years, he would have the same hairline as his father. Knowing this gave me *so* much pleasure.

"Cortés," he said firmly, "my office now." Turning around, he walked to the room.

I shot Jackie a look of confusion, and she shrugged.

I entered his office, closing the door behind me. The room was minimalist, with a clean desk which had a laptop and a nameplate on it, with a few framed degrees hung on the wall. The view of the surrounding buildings coming through the window in front of me wasn't dull.

Sitting in the chair across from him, I tried to mimic his stony gaze. "What can I help you with, Mr. McAdams?"

"I have a job offer for you," he said curtly.

I sat up straighter, crossing my ankles over one another. "A job offer? You sure get right to the point, huh?" *Here I'd thought I was getting fired.*

"You know I don't believe in jibber-jabber," he said. "My associate wanted me to expand our magazine with a purely online sister magazine called ... *According to Staci and Greg.* It'll revolve around perspectives from men and women, how they view the world in different ways. It'll show each side of the relationship, outlining common miscommunications that come from it. Of course, you can explore many avenues with this topic, but that will be your starting point."

"When you say explore many avenues —"

"Here at Nast Publishing, our articles only pertain to relationships, sex, careers, self-improvement, celebrities, fashion, and beauty. If you stick to those parameters, we are good, Miss Cortés."

"And when you say associate, what do you mean by that?"

"My son."

"Greg?" I asked.

"No, Jamie."

For the love of God, there's another one?

"My son Greg wants no part in running the company. He seems happy in being a writer." He spat out the word *writer* like it was beneath him.

Mr. McAdams stared at me; the awkward silence told me it was my turn to talk.

"Wow, this sounds like a great opportunity, but this magazine … it's exactly what I'm already doing." I cleared my throat to flush out the sarcasm and tried again. "So, what does this mean? Am I getting my own magazine?"

"You'll be in charge of writing articles for our biweekly issues while running a discussion forum for men and women asking advice. You'll also respond to any comments or questions related to the issues you produce. I'll have final say, and Kate will over-look things, but, yes, you'll have full control of the creativity. This magazine is supposed to be active with reader connections. Seeing as you're single and in the know with today's challenges of dating in a big city, I thought you'd be the perfect fit."

Who knew being single would be an asset? I'd thought he was promoting me based on my writing skills. Either way, it still was a good thing. At least I wasn't getting fired.

"Thank you, Mr. McAdams," I said, almost breathless. "This is a lot more responsibility, which is exactly what I've been looking for." I stood, shaking his hand, eager to get started. "Will I get paid more for this?" I asked.

"I have to discuss it with Jamie, and of course, Kate will fill you in during the next couple of days."

In other words, I wouldn't be getting paid much more than I already was.

Then, a thought crossed my mind, and I slowly sank back into the seat. "If there will be both men and women perspectives ... I'll be working with Greg on this?"

"Yes, Greg McAdams, my son," he said.

Oh, joy.

Of course, the whole *According to Staci and Greg* should have been self-explanatory, but I was so worried about being let go that it didn't faze me. Oh, but it was fazing me now. *Was. It. Ever.*

"You'll co-write every issue with Greg, working in the small conference room across the hall. It's a good idea to run a blog of your own as well to pump out the articles, to get readers sucked into the website ..."

Mr. McAdams droned on about his ideas for the magazine while I sat there, speechless, running Greg's name through my mind, and my muscles cramped.

How on earth will I be able to work with that man? Does Greg know?

It jolted me back to reality when Mr. McAdams Senior yelled out my name.

Shaking my head, I said, "With all due respect, Mr. McAdams, I know he's your son, but I don't think Greg has anything of value to contribute on the topic of relationships and dating."

"Nonsense," he said, tapping his fingers on the desk. "He's the top columnist at *Avant-Garde*, so it only fits that you two work together. I want you to go over there right now and introduce yourself. Get started on a full proposal for the magazine while the IT department finishes up the final designs for the site. I'll need at least thirty short blog posts, spread out throughout the next few weeks, including the weekend, but only in the beginning to increase readership. Go now! We can't have bored readers for a site that hasn't started yet. Get out of my office!"

My knees shook as I stumbled out of the room. When I got to my cubicle, I collapsed in my chair.

"What's wrong?" Jackie asked. "You look pale, which is saying a lot, considering your flawless tan skin. Puerto Ricans are lucky. My skin is so pasty," she said, studying herself in a compact mirror.

I was also half-Cuban, but I didn't have time to get into that.

"Jackie," I huffed, "I got a new job."

"That's great!" she squealed, clapping her hands.

"It's with Greg."

Jackie frowned as she crouched next to me, placing a hand on mine. "Does it mean we won't work together anymore?"

We usually did our brainstorming together, and sometimes, Jackie used me as her guinea pig to test out products for her research, which was always fun, except for the last time. I'd gotten a rash using anti-aging cream, but I still took one for the team. Anything for Jackie.

"I'll still be around," I said, swallowing hard, realizing I was taking on more than I was capable of handling. "But much of my time will be spent with Greg while we get the online magazine off the ground. I'm supposed to go over there now." I stared at the door across the hall.

Jackie turned my gaze back to her, pinching my chin. "This is your job," she said, and I knew I'd be getting a lecture. "You're going to march in there—so swallow your pride. I don't care if you don't like Greg, but you will work with him to make the best damn magazine in the world!"

"But, Jackie—"

"No," she said, dragging me out of my seat, pushing me towards the door. "March, young lady."

I took a few hesitant steps before looking over my shoulder. Jackie stood behind me with her hands on her hips.

"No wonder your kids are so moody," I huffed before making my way to the entrance.

Across the hall, I looked through the glass door into the *Avant-Garde* office. It wasn't much different from *Starlet*. People were dressed in semi-casual wear, rushing around the room, chatting with coffee in their hands. They clustered in their cliques like a bunch of high school girls. Deep chuckles echoed through the office.

As I gripped the handle of the glass door, I closed my eyes and took a deep breath. With one quick movement, I swung the door open and stomped through the office like I owned the place. Or would have, but I tripped over the carpet in front of the receptionist's desk. With whatever dignity I had left, I stood up and smiled at Debbie, the receptionist. Thank God no one else was around, like Greg.

When I entered the conference room without another hitch, I slapped my notebook on the table after closing the blinds, then waited in the office chair.

A short second later, Greg came in with two cups of coffee. "There you are, I've been looking all over for you. Jackie told me you were in here waiting." He placed a paper cup in front of me. "You drink coffee, right?" If he knew me better, he would know I didn't, but I guessed I should give him some credit. Greg didn't remember me. Then again, I looked different from the last time I'd seen him, which was six years ago.

I slouched deeper into my chair, crossing my arms.

"I guess that's your way of telling me you want to get started?" Greg asked.

"Sit down."

Then, I shook my head as he proceeded to sit next to me. Seeing this, he laughed and went to the seat across from me.

"So, I assume your boss—my father—filled you in on the project we'll be heading together?"

"Let me get one thing clear," I said, pushing the coffee away from me. "I am not here by choice. You are a means to an end—to further my career. To produce this magazine, we will work together no more than we have to. Once we're done getting this off the ground, we will part ways and work in our own offices. We will only coordinate by e-mail. We will not form a professional or personal relationship. Got it?"

"Are you done?" Greg smirked, folding his hands on the table. "Because I'd like to get started without dealing with whatever anger you're holding onto toward me."

"Don't flatter yourself, Greg," I said, squirming in my chair. "If I had any anger toward you, then that would mean you meant something— which you don't."

He chuckled. "What did I do to you?" He stared at me with his palms turned upward in a shrug.

I looked into his eyes, wanting nothing more than to pluck the perfectly placed hairs on his head out one by one. "Your father—my boss," I said quickly, looking at my notepad, "wants us to get a proposal for the direction of the site done by the end of the week. I can handle writing that up. For today, I think we can just bounce around ideas for articles and the daily blog posts."

"Right, the blog posts," he said, still staring at me. He leaned back in his chair before he pulled out his cell phone. "This magazine is supposed to engage readers practically every second of the day. I think we should hire some social media influencers to promote our blog posts to broaden our readership." He turned his phone screen to me, which displayed the profile of a famous YouTube star. "He's a good friend of mine, and he has been freelancing for *Avant-Garde* for years. I think he'll be a good fit for our team."

Snatching the phone, I scrolled through the information and nodded, pleasantly surprised. "I think this is a great idea. Set up a meeting so I can share my thoughts with your friend on the articles he should write."

"Well," he replied, putting his phone in his pocket, "I don't think we should look for a ghostwriter when the whole point of this magazine is to promote us—as a male and female point of view about dating in this generation. That's why my father is pushing so hard for us to be involved in the comment section. We need to interact with our readers."

"Who was talking about ghostwriters? I meant the post he would write about us. I want to approve everything before it's published on his social media. We have to be picky about who we align ourselves with in case they don't agree with the message we're sending," I said, jotting down a few articles ideas.

"Everyone wants to create healthy relationships, but I don't think censorship is the right way to go," he said under his breath.

What was he talking about?

Ignoring his comment, I turned my paper to him, full of titles like:

"How to Increase Intimacy"

"Trust-Building Exercises"

"How to Get Back into Dating"

"What's New in the Dating Pool?"

"Obviously, we need to brainstorm catchier titles, but the main theme is here. Empowering people with information, so they don't waste their time while searching for the right person. It's not about getting the guy or girl. It's about forming a healthy, lasting relationship with someone."

"I agree," he said, tossing the paper back.

I raised my eyebrows. "You agree?"

"Yes, you have some great ideas. I like the direction you want to take it. But we also need something edgy to bring in more readers."

"Such as?"

"I don't know yet." He tapped his hand on the desk, then leaned back in his chair. "We live in a time that makes it challenging to be present in anything. We are addicted to novelty, and now, with these dating apps, it's like a wide buffet of options. It reduces your willingness to settle on what might be the right person for you, so you don't because you think there might be someone better out there, but it doesn't materialize in practice. People don't understand you need to invest time to get something out of a relationship."

"You believe that? Investing time in a relationship?" I blinked.

"Of course, if the person is worth it." He paused. "But I think people jump ship before really getting to know someone."

"Huh," I said. "I'm impressed by that outlook."

"I'm not just a pretty face," he said with a wink.

"You're not even that," I grumbled, looking down at my notes. When my gaze lifted, it was met with provocative eyes. I cleared my throat. "So, how do we get the readers to give us their time? What would be different from the relationship section in *Starlet* or *Avant-Garde?*"

"We will be different because we'll give it a personal touch. Dating is tenuous and hard, but it can also be fun. We will give our readers the tools to date smart."

For the next couple of hours, we discussed article ideas, web design, and our proposal for our bosses. Both had to sign off on everything before we could continue. Soon, *According to Staci and Greg* had some legs to stand on. It pained me that we worked so well together, but when he wasn't so smug, he had some good ideas. For a while, I could put aside my pride, be civil with him, except for a few witty exchanges.

I could feel when it was time for lunch, as my stomach rumbled. My brain started shutting off the Good Ideas tap. "I think we should end it here for today," I said, moving out of my chair. "Mornings will be good for this so that I can work on my articles in the afternoons. Sounds good?" I stood, but before I could reach the door, Greg was holding it open for me. "I can get it myself," I said flatly.

"I'm a gentleman. It's just how I am." He grinned.

I took the door handle from him before stomping back to my office. When I returned to my desk, Jackie smiled in a way that made my cheeks go hot.

"So, how was it?" she asked, rolling her chair over to me. "Was Greg as charming as ever? Can you imagine if you two had kids? They would be so gorgeous."

My stomach turned. "Don't you dare say that again, or I'll start dry-heaving." I turned to my computer but felt Jackie staring at me. Sighing, I whirled back around, rolling closer to her. "Okay, we shared our thoughts for the magazine and discussed our game plan. He had some great ideas, and he agreed with a lot of what I said. Happy?"

"See? You worried for nothing. Greg is a great guy if you give him a chance."

I leaned close to her ear, whispering, "I'll tell you something, but if it ever gets out, I'll know you blabbed."

"I would never," she said with a severe expression, crossing her heart with one finger.

"Today, with Greg, I had fu ... fu ..."

Jackie smiled from ear to ear. "Are you saying what I think you're saying?"

"I had fun," I said, the last word sliding out of my mouth like vomit.

Jackie clapped lightly, struggling to hold back her squealing. "I knew you guys would hit it off."

"It wasn't like that," I hissed. Then, I softened my tone to give Jackie an apologetic look. "Yes, Greg was charming, intelligent, and he used big words ..."

"But?"

"But that's his ploy!" I rolled back to my desk. "He entices women with his charm, then scratches another notch in his bedpost when he's done. He's a player. I refuse to fall for his advances."

"Wait, he put the moves on you?" Jackie frowned.

"Ew, no," I said, looking up at her. "But, if Greg ever tries anything, I won't fall for it. He's a user." I took out my agenda from my bottom drawer before slapping it on my desk. "He thinks people are disposable once he's taken all he can from them."

Like Luis.

Jackie leaned on my desk, her arms folded. "Has he ever done those things to you?"

"He doesn't have to," I said, staring straight at my computer screen. "I know him well enough to understand the type of man he is," I said, typing furiously on my keyboard.

"Try not to be too hard on him," she said. "You wouldn't want it to affect your work because you couldn't get along."

Her words sat in my mind for the rest of the day. She was right. I couldn't let the anger I had to project on my work. I had to express myself in other ways so the magazine didn't suffer. As I left for work that day, a sly grin remained plastered on my face. My mind swirled with ideas. Just because I didn't like him didn't mean I couldn't have fun with Greg. Right?

I knew exactly what to do.

66

Want to get rid of a man? Be a crazy. Hot. Mess. Guys get put off by drama, and that's the most successful way to purge a man from your life faster than you can type out #boybye. I get it— you're the coolest girl on the planet, and that's why he's so into you. Flip the switch, make him believe you're a complete natural disaster.

So the next time you see him, try this one out on him: Sorry I'm late. I was trying to sneak out of my apartment without my landlord catching me. I'm, like, two months behind on my rent. Then, on my way here, my car broke down, and I had to steal a bicycle to get here. I'm so thirsty I could drink a bottle of Chianti, but none of that cheap kind—you're paying, right?

You get the gist.

99

5 Ways to Make a Guy Leave You Alone
by Staci Cortés

3

STACI

THE NEXT MORNING, I did something I'd never thought was possible. I got to work early. I was stepping into the elevator as Greg was coming through the revolving doors of the building. We caught a glimpse of each other as the doors started to close. With one last attempt, Greg held up his hand, yelling at me to keep it open, but it was too late. The elevators were extremely slow, so waiting for one was excruciating.

When the doors opened, I made a beeline for the conference room after I waved at Jackie through the window. I sat in the same chair as yesterday, scribbling notes and waiting for Greg to arrive. I kept my head down until I heard the door open. I lifted my head. If looks could kill, I would be dead right now. *Mission accomplished.*

"You're late," I smiled as he tried to catch his breath, most likely from running the long lobby.

"No thanks to you. I had to wait ten minutes for the elevator," he said, flopping down in the seat across from me. "Didn't you see me running for the elevator?"

I scrunched my lips, tapping the pen on my chin. "No, I don't think so." I fluttered my eyelashes.

"I was calling your name," he said, pulling his laptop out of his suitcase. "Oh well. I guess you were so wrapped up in whatever that beautiful mind cooks up every day."

"Wouldn't you like to know?" I snorted.

He reclined in his chair. "Oh, yeah, I would love to get in that head of yours. You fascinate me," he said, taking a sip from his coffee without removing his eyes from my face.

"Can you stop?" I said.

"What?"

"Looking at me. It makes me uncomfortable."

He smiled, straining his tie. "Where did you go to school? You have an approach to your column I've never seen with writers."

"What's that supposed to mean?" I snapped.

"Relax, it was a compliment." He chuckled. "You're blunt with your information, and you don't often use any bias to sway people. You state your opinion while presenting the facts in a balanced way. No matter how many people comment on your articles about you being too harsh, you don't change who you are. You're strong, and that clearly shows in your work."

"What? Have you been reading up on me?"

"Of course," he said with a bright smile. "I always research the people I work with. Don't you?"

"I didn't have to," I said, handing him a copy of the proposal. "I wanted to have your say on this before we submitted it. Maybe you can add something to it that I forgot."

Greg took it, skimming through the pages. "I trust you. It looks good. What did you mean you didn't have to research me?"

"When I was younger, I had a summer job working at the Pelham Country Club. I used to work with your cousin Josh."

"Yeah, I used to go there sometimes," he said. "How come I don't remember you?"

"I remember you—vividly, in fact."

He sat there staring at me, deep in thought. "To be honest," he said, scratching the back of his neck, "I've blacked out most of those days. If I wasn't drinking or smoking weed, I was living recklessly. It's a miracle I'm still here."

"Look at you now. A changed man?"

"I am," he said. "After my motorcycle accident, I did some soul searching while traveling through Europe and South America. Experiencing different cultures and seeing how some people lived in poverty opened my eyes to the world. One day, I'd like to write a piece about my experience from the perspective of my younger self and now. You're from South America, right?"

"My mother is Cuban, my father is Puerto Rican," I said, disturbed that my body had a warm, fuzzy feeling from his story. "I was born here, but my parents got married in Florida. Then, we somehow ended up in New York. This is the only home I've known."

"I'd love to interview your parents if that's okay?" he said, his gaze caught mine. "I'm working on a project."

I smiled, then quickly wiped it away. "My parents would love to be interviewed. They're always telling stories of their childhood. It'd be great for them to share those stories with someone else for a change."

"Do you think you could set that up?" he asked, leaning in very closely, making me feel uncomfortable. *Why did he have to be so attractive?*

"I mean, I don't want to push, but now that I've said my idea out loud, it'd be great to get started."

"How are you going to publish it? Your magazine isn't exactly the platform for it."

"I'll figure it out when I finish it," Greg said.

I looked up at him, seeing a spark of excitement in his eyes. In this light, his eyes were like the ocean sparkling in the sunlight. I pushed that thought away as I cleared my throat. "Sure, I could set it up for you. I'll give my dad your number. Pass me your phone and I'll plug the number in for you."

What am I getting myself into?

"Great!" he said, clapping once. "What about you? What piece would you write if you could?"

"Don't we have work to do?"

"We've got time to kill until the social media influencers get here for the interviews."

I dropped my pen. "Multiple interviews? I thought I was just meeting your freelance friend?"

"We got talking last night, and he connected me with a bunch of people. Options are good, right? Now, answer the question."

"Fine," I sighed. "I'd want to write a piece about this foundation, Worldly Education. They're not well-known but they build schools and bring supplies to villages all over Africa and Asia. They're trying to expand to the rest of the world. Someone needs to shine a spotlight on the work they're doing. The piece is almost done, but Kate won't publish it in *Starlet*, which is fine because I want it in the *New York Times*."

Greg whistled. "That's an impressive goal."

"I've wanted to work there since I was four when I saw the magazine in a dentist's office, the one with Brad Pitt on the cover with the headline, 'America's Fascination with Buddhism.' I didn't know how to read, but even at that age, I just knew it was an influential magazine." I smiled to myself. "I actually cried when my mom took it away from me."

"I remember the cover. *Seven Years in Tibet*—have you ever seen the movie?"

"Yes, many times," I said.

With the way he was looking at me, I felt the heat run up the back of my neck. Why did he have this effect on me? One minute, I wanted to strangle him—*so badly,* and the next, I wanted to ...

Well, just leave it there, Staci.

"Staci Cortés, editor-in-chief of *New York Times* magazine," he said, fanning his arms across an invisible banner. "I like the sound of that. You're almost overqualified for the position."

"Oh, please," I scoffed, trying to hold back my smile. "When did you get to be such a suck-up?"

"It's true. You're an educated, classy woman. I'd hate to see your talents go to waste in a relationship column for the rest of your life."

"It's good work. I help people." That was what I kept telling myself.

"I'm not saying it isn't, but I've got a feeling you're destined for much more."

We locked eyes, caught in a staring match of mutual appreciation. When a fist tapped on the glass door, we broke our gaze and glanced at it. The influencers were here, and I was eager to know about their visions for the magazine, but leaving Greg to deal with it on his own was much more fun. This would keep him busy at least for the next two hours, giving me a head start on writing my first post.

"Well, I'll leave you to it then," I said, standing abruptly.

"Excuse me?" he asked as I ushered everyone into the conference room.

"I trust your instincts. Let me know who you pick," I said.

"These interviews will take me all day!"

Oh, I was counting on it.

"Have fun!" I winked.

LATER, I headed to the break room for an herbal tea. I grabbed a tea bag from the cupboard in the white room that smelled musty, then opened the fridge to look for the snack I'd packed. What I found instead was Greg's lunch, placed neatly in a container. I wasn't hungry enough for a full meal, but I wanted to piss Greg off, so I pulled out a chair across the linoleum floor and ate a soggy tuna sandwich with the apple slices.

Did a kid pack his lunch?

Once I polished it off, Greg came in, looking drained. He stopped at the edge of the table, rubbing his face. "I put my name on that for a reason."

He appeared annoyed, but he struggled not to show it.

"Oh, I'm sorry," I said, innocently batting my eyelashes. "I didn't see that. I was just looking for something to eat."

I waited for Greg to lose his temper, but he sighed.

"My niece made my lunch. She was staying with me for the night to give her parents a break. I was looking forward to it. How was it?"

Awful, but I needed to push the knife deeper into his back. "It was so delicious," I said, wiping my mouth on a napkin. "You should have tried some. How are the interviews going?"

"Fine. Shouldn't you be doing something useful?" Greg said in a calm tone that irked me.

"I'm going to start drafting some articles for the blog posts. I don't need to be here for that, but I think I'll bring my laptop into the conference room so we can get to know each other." I grinned as he said nothing.

For the rest of the day, I tried to be as annoying as possible. I constantly cleared my throat, interrupting his interviews, and played music from my laptop. But nothing was annoying him.

OVER THE NEXT WEEK, I wanted to break him. So I got to work early and rearranged his office furniture. I threw away or ate his food and flirted with all his coworkers to make him jealous. I wore girlie perfumes that overwhelmed the room. I was unbelievably irritating—yet he wouldn't break.

It was like trying to crack a code.

"Can you believe that guy?" I asked Jackie as we sat in our usual booth at the bar.

"'Reveal Her Sex Appeal with a Palm Reading,'" I read the title from my phone. It was an article Greg had written for *Avant-Garde* last month. "Is he for real? Who reads this crap?"

"Um, men," Jackie added.

"See what I have to work with? He knows nothing about women. This magazine is going to tank, and it'll have my name attached to it," I said, deflated.

"You think making his life difficult will make things easier for you?"

Jackie is such a killjoy.

"Sure, but it makes no difference anyway. He just takes everything I throw at him without a second thought. He's so damn agreeable. Like, yesterday, I brought thirty mylar balloons into the conference room, and he acted like they weren't there. I sent him spam e-mails, I talked on the phone to my sister like a teenager," I scoffed.

"Are you trying to get rid of him or get fired?" Her eyebrows went up.

"Fired? No. I'm an asset to Nast Publishing. Mr. McAdams Senior would never ... would he?"

"You said it yourself. One day, Greg will run the show."

Jackie had a point. Maybe I was overdoing it.

What was wrong with me? I was not usually like this. Why did Greg bring out the worst in me?

"What?" I asked.

Jackie blankly stared at me. "All I asked was if you were going to order another drink," she said softly.

"Oh. No, thanks," I said. "And another thing—"

"Okay, I get it!" she yelped, throwing her hands up. "You've been talking about Greg nonstop since we got here. *Greg is this and that. Greg did something annoying. I hate Greg.* I get it! As much as I adore the guy, we never talked about him this much before. I've had enough." She downed a shot of tequila, slamming the glass on the table.

"I'm sorry," I said. "I'll stop. Wait, I have one last thing to say!"

"Don't." She scowled. "No more talking. It's my turn. You're going to listen to me talk about my kids and their father. Got it?"

I nodded. *Jeez, what was her problem?*

I'd never seen Jackie get so upset. *Have I been talking too much about Greg?*

That was because I hated him, right? But, when a woman talked too much about a man, it could only mean one thing. I had suspected the line that had me loathing him was thinning out every time I spent time with Greg.

No, it can't be.

I was too mortified to speak for the rest of the night. Not because I was afraid of Jackie—though she could be scary, like I'd just learned—but I was petrified of something I never imagined I would ever do.

Fall for Greg McAdams.

> Does she have daggers in her eyes every time she sees you? Chances are, she probably hates your guts, but there's still a chance you could turn things around, that Is, if you play your cards right.
>
> Step one: figure out why she wishes you'd disappeared from the face of the earth. Did you do something that made her upset? Chances are the answer is yes.
>
> Step two: talk to her and find common ground. Getting her to open up and talk about herself will only trigger her curiosity to know more about you, and hopefully get her to see you as a person who's not hate-worthy.

How to Talk to a Woman Who Hates You
by Greg McAdams

4

STACI

THE NEXT DAY, I headed for the revolving door of the office
building and spotted Greg standing next to his new toy—a Harley
—with his arms crossed. He wore a leather jacket, a red shirt, and
dark denim jeans.

"Hardly work attire," I said over my shoulders as I walked
away in my dress pants and a new chiffon blouse.

"Staci, listen," he said firmly. "I don't know what I've done to
make you hate me, but the way you have been acting isn't the real
you. I've seen how you care for Jackie. I've witnessed your warm
nature around the office. You're a good person, so today, I will
make you show me that person."

Oh brother, not a chance.

"You've been observing me?"

"One has to around you. You're a wild creature. Never know
when the claws might come out." The corner of his mouth
twitched.

"Hilarious."

"Get on the bike. This is a company retreat." He tossed me a
helmet, and I caught it.

"Good reflexes." Greg smiled.

"Why would I get on that thing?"

"Because, deep down, you're an adventurous person," he said, his smile making my skin tingle. "I know you're eager to ride with me. You've been eyeing it after work all week. What do you say?"

"Why does it bother you if I like you or not?"

"Because everybody likes me."

I let out a breath. "You keep believing that. We have work to do."

"Well, despite your best efforts to distract me, I've finished more than enough work to please my father and your boss, Kate. Will you come, please? A couple of hours. That's it." He stuck out his bottom lip then held his hand.

Cute.

Maybe this is what we needed. Who knows, after today I might have a different opinion of Greg. I guessed he could grow on me, like an acquired taste.

"Fine, you win," I said.

I pulled on the helmet and hopped behind him on the bike without another word. He revved it up before we zoomed down the street, zigzagging between several cars. A rush of adrenaline exploded through me. He was going so fast I had to hold on to his waist, but when I did that, he reached down and brought my hand higher on his chest, placing his hand on top for what seemed like an eternity before returning it on the bar of his motorcycle. Why was Greg so touchy-feely? I wished I hadn't enjoyed it so much.

OUR FIRST STOP was at a duck pond in Central Park. We sat beside each other on the bench, talking about our families and throwing breadcrumbs at the quacking creatures splashing in the water.

"I talked to your mom on the phone yesterday," Greg said, eating a sandwich he had bought us at the corner food truck. "Your mother is an amazing woman. She inspired me to make the piece longer than I'd planned. She even gave me the numbers of her friends who might be interested in talking to me."

"Did you tell her you were single?" I giggled.

"I don't think so."

"Did she ask you if you were married?"

He nodded. "Oddly, yes."

"Those numbers she gave you are of friends whose daughters are single. She's trying to set you up."

His mouth fell open. "No ... your mom wouldn't do that. "

"You don't know my mother."

I laughed until he brushed the hair away from my face. I felt something shifting in his eyes, something profound.

"Okay, truth time," he announced, standing in front of me. "Why do you hate me so much?"

"I don't hate you *per se* ... just a little annoyed," I said, standing to walk around the pond.

He followed beside me with his hands in his pockets. "Then why have you been acting like a brat?"

"I'm not a brat!" I squealed.

"You licked my muffin the other day, so I couldn't eat it. At least have the decency to eat it."

"I would have, but I didn't want the calories," I mused, but he gave me a flat look.

"You're a very disturbed woman," he muttered.

"Okay," I sighed, stopping to stare at the shimmering water. "I'll admit, with you, I revert to this immature self, but getting to know you ... the more I like you as a friend. And that was ... unexpected." I almost bit my tongue after saying those words, but it was the truth.

"Then why not apologize?"

He stood behind me, and when I turned around, the hurt in his eyes made my gut twist in knots.

"I guess holding on to my anger kept me ... distant." Distant enough that I would never get hurt again.

"That still doesn't explain the way you've been acting," he said with a smirk. "You're a beautiful, intelligent woman. You don't need to hold on to whatever hurt you had in the past."

There was something about Greg that made me want to open up, but I didn't want him to judge me—afraid to show my real self.

"I was rounder when I was younger," I said blatantly, staring at my feet. "I told you once, I worked at the Pelham Country Club," I said as he nodded. "There was this guy I liked who used to come there often. I developed a major crush on him."

"And I remind you of that guy?" He frowned.

My eyes dragged across his face. I couldn't believe he didn't remember. He touched my shoulder, and I slowly backed away.

"We should get back to the office. I have much work to do."

———

MY LUNCH with Greg had given me an idea to pitch for my next article — "Five Signs You Are Moving Forward." Greg had made me realized I had some emotional history I needed to sort out, and maybe my readers did, too. I was not the only woman on earth who had had her heart squashed. These painful experiences got recognition for the way we behaved without realizing it. I'd always thought I'd moved on from Luis or any other man hurting me, but there were visible signs I hadn't. Maybe my readers and I could both learn from this. I had been typing my pitch when two tickets appeared in front of my face. My gaze slowly followed up the steady hand that was attached to a muscular arm. The man was relentless in his mission —I wasn't going to get anything accomplished today.

"What do you want, Greg?" I let out a breath.

"I have two tickets to watch the Knicks at Madison Square Garden," he said. "Want to come?"

"I don't like sports." I continued typing without meeting his gaze.

"What kind of New Yorker are you?"

"The kind who has a deadline to meet." I flashed him a look of annoyance.

"It's tonight."

"No, thanks. I'm busy." I informed Greg.

"Doing what?"

"Scrubbing the dirt out of my kitchen tiles." I flashed him a smile, and he gave me a flat look.

"What if I told you it was work-related?" He perked an eyebrow.

"You don't know how to let things go," I huffed.

"Persistence is my worst and best quality." He grinned.

"I've noticed," I said, snatching the tickets out of his hand. "Okay." I leaned back in my chair, making it roll back an inch or two. "I'm listening,"

"What if our first post for the magazine is about a couple who's on a date at a Knicks game?"

He smiled, and I rolled my eyes, going back to my e-mail.

"I know what you're trying to do. It's not going to work."

"Let me finish." He continued when he had my full attention, "We'll go on pretend dates and keep a diary about it. I'm sure we'll have enough material between us. It will be a post about a date with two viewpoints, like *he said, she said* kind of thing?"

"Or *she said, he said*," I volunteered.

"Sure, whatever makes you happy." His eyes met mine; I diverted them back to the tickets. "It would give our readers insight into our minds."

"Your mind? Now, that's a scary thought," I murmured, and he chuckled.

"Admit it— it's a great idea," he said, leaning forward.

"But I have a better idea."

"Okay, let's hear it." He sat at the corner of my desk.

My eyes met his, and that smile was dreamy. For a second, I wondered what it would be like to kiss that mouth.

I've gone mad. Seriously, stop staring, Staci!

I needed space. I was spending way too much time with Greg McAdams.

I cleared my throat. "Let's pitch *According to Staci* this way. I'll be a wing-girl for men. I'm giving them an insight into what women think and want from a man. Teaching them what not to do on a date or in a relationship," I said, lifting my hands to the sides.

"But you forgot one thing."

"What's that?"

"It's *According to Staci and Greg*. You and I are the brands. However, I see what you're saying; I'll be catering to the female readers. Advising women looking for Mr. Right." He nodded his head.

"Yeah, sure. That would work, too." I shrugged, pulling out my pad of paper to jot some ideas down. "Maybe this might be better for you. I think you have a higher success rate, helping out women than men."

"What?" He frowned.

"Have you read your articles? You know nothing about women." A clicking noise came out of my mouth, and I pointed my finger at him like I was pulling the trigger on him.

"You don't know what you're saying. I know women." The side of his mouth lifted.

"You don't know me."

"No, that's for sure." He tapped my desk with his hand and got up. "You, Staci Cortés, are not like other women, not by a long shot."

"I'll take it as a compliment."

"You should," he said as his eyes dragged down to my crossed bare legs, lingering there a moment before meeting my eyes. "But, for the sake of the magazine, I think we should stick to *she said, he said* kind of thing."

"Why don't we speak to your dad? See what he thinks?" I thought he was doing this all wrong.

"I don't need to. *According to Staci and Greg* is my project. Especially now that my good-for-nothing brother Jamie is in California."

"I thought—"

"I know what you thought. I knew you wouldn't be on board if you knew I had full control of this magazine."

"So, what, this makes you my boss?"

"Yes," he replied.

"Why would you choose me? Knowing we are not fond of each other?" I shuddered. "Why not Julia or Jackie?"

"Because you're the best writer we have," Greg said.

I felt a tickle in my stomach. *Greg thought I was a good writer?*

"Who said I wasn't fond of you?" His eyes met mine.

I had been so preoccupied on hating this man that I could only assume the feeling was mutual. Maybe that was the plan all along. If Greg weren't attracted to me, then I would be clear of getting hurt again.

"All right, I can't believe I'm agreeing to this. I'll meet you there," I said.

He snatched the tickets from me. "You don't want me to pick you up?"

"No, I will leave from work. Some of us still have a deadline to meet," I said, going back to my e-mail, hoping Greg got the hint and went away.

"Okay, just don't be late." He smacked the tickets across his palm, like he'd just scored a point.

"Hold on. So we're clear, it's not a date, it's work," I said.

"Sure, but there's something I want to get off my chest, too."

"Yeah, what's that?"

"I don't put out on the first date, just in case you get funny ideas," he said.

Before I could say anything, he walked off, disappearing through the glass doors.

> **"** When a man goes above and beyond to make sure your needs are taken care of before his own, he does it because he wants to make you happy. He knows that's the only way he can keep you around. **"**

When He Knows You're the One
by Staci Cortés

5

STACI

"YOU REALIZE the game has already started," Greg said, standing at the front door of Madison Square Garden with his arms crossed in front of his chest.

"Sorry, I lost track of time," I said, stumbling out of the taxicab, making my way toward him.

After going through the checkpoint, we found our seats, then Greg took off to get us something to drink. I had to admit I didn't expect Greg to be a total gentleman. Of course it was an act, and I wondered what crazy antics I could pull off tonight to get him to show me his true side—an overbearing, pompous jerk that he was. Five minutes later Greg's voice stirs me out of my thoughts. When my eyes met Greg, holding a tray of fast food—which I didn't eat ... I realized the potential.

This was going to be fun.

"What did I miss?" he said, handing me a hot dog and a Coke.

I hesitated for a second. "Thanks, but I don't eat that stuff," I said.

He looked at me, confused.

"Sorry, I should have said something before." I shrugged.

"Okay, so what can I get you?"

"Do they make salads?" I smiled shyly.

He let out a long breath. "You're very demanding, Miss Cortés."

"Oh, it's okay. I'll get something else," I said, getting up, making my way around him, but a wall of his broad chest prevented me from going further.

"Here, hold this." Greg handed me his food. "Let me go back, see what else they have," he said.

I could feel his frustration. Who thought irritating Greg would be so much fun? I never promised I would play nice, yet Greg had acted like the perfect gentleman. I wondered what it would take or how far I could push until he cracked. Then, he'd have no choice but to take me off this project, then I can go back to *Starlet* until I was ready to move on to something else.

———

LATER—WAY later—Greg came back, holding in one hand a white plastic bag with a purple logo that had *Andy's Gourmet Salads* written on it.

"What's that?" I asked as he took the seat next to me.

"Your salads—as in plural. I wasn't sure what you liked, so I bought the avocado salad and the Asian sesame vinaigrette. Take your pick, sweetheart." He held out two clear plastic containers.

"I didn't know they sold Andy's Gourmet at the food court."

"They don't," he said, meeting my eyes.

"You went out?" I said, knowing the game had already started and he had missed twenty minutes of it.

"Don't say I do nothing for you."

I couldn't believe he had gone through the trouble, but then again, he probably wanted me to write about our date, making him out to be the swoon-worthy guy.

"I'll have the avocado. Thank you," I said. After a moment of silence, I asked, "So, doesn't your father have a suite here?"

"Yes, he does—up there, just below the bridge level."

"*Oh*. Why aren't we sitting there?" I asked. I looked around. I wasn't sure if these were the best seats in the house, but I guessed not since we were far from court level.

"Because I didn't want you to accuse me of showing off. Anyhow, I knew it wouldn't impress you."

"And you know what would?"

"I'm awesome; it should be enough." He winked, and I snorted.

"That's why you're single." I dug into my salad.

His eyes scanned the court before meeting mine again. "I'm single because I choose to be. I'm looking for the one."

"The one *right* now, you mean," I added.

"Nope, the one and only. What's so funny?" He cast a look my way.

"Oh, come on, Greg. You write about how to pick up girls at the bar or which lingerie to buy your girlfriend for Valentine's Day," I said, playing with my food with my plastic fork. "You wouldn't be able to write those articles if you didn't think you were a ladies' man."

He looked at me. "This coming from a woman whose last article was called 'Seven Lap Dance Moves to Make Men Melt.'"

"Okay, but—"

"*Okay* what? You think you're any different?" he asked. "Don't judge me, we're in the same boat."

I wondered how he could say that. I'd spent most of my childhood in a small apartment in Jackson Heights, raised in a bilingual home. Greg McAdams's life had been spent living in a big house with an au pair. His parents never had to worry about money as mine did.

He was trying hard to get on my good side because, if he thought there was no difference between us, then he was dreaming in Technicolor.

"The one, huh?" I said. "That's a fairy tale idea."

"I don't think so."

I shot Greg a look. "I didn't take you for the sappy, romantic kind."

"I'm not. It's from my experience that made me want to believe in it more. I come from a broken home. My father married twice, and my mother is going on her third in a few months. I have to wonder if they settled too fast," he said, his eyes focus on the court. "I never had anything in my life that was stable. I don't want that for my children, which I'll hopefully have one day. I want to do better for them than what my parents did for my siblings and me." He glanced back, catching me staring. "What's that look for?"

"That's sweet."

I never believed in fate or the *one*. It always felt like a mythological concept, but now, sitting next to this man, sharing his ideas about family and love, it had me wishing for it.

"So, you read my article?" I said, the first to break away from our gaze.

"Of course. All of them. My favorite is 'How to Be More Playful with Your Boyfriend,' especially number three—the slap and tickle," he said, and I laughed. "If you're ever looking for a candidate to try these things out, I'm your man." He pointed to his chest with his thumb.

I slowly looked him over. "Well, you could use some slapping."

He chuckled. "All jokes aside, I'm a man who's doing his job," he said. I had the urge to roll my eyes, but I held off until he finished what he had to say. "I don't believe in half of the things I write."

"So, why do it?"

"Because I'm hoping to set myself up for something better."

"Can't Daddy open some doors?"

"Sure—tomorrow morning if I want. But what good would that be? No, I want to earn things on my merit," he said with his eyes on the game.

I stared at him when he wasn't looking. I had to admit, I admired him for that, not wanting to take full advantage of the McAdams name.

"Do you ever come here with your dad?"

"No, not unless it's a corporate event or we're entertaining clients. My dad is not even a fan of the sport." He shrugged. "To be honest, he never brought me to a basketball game. My father was always busy building Nast Publishing," he added.

My stomach clenched. Maybe Greg had missed out on a lot of things growing up. My family hadn't come from money, but my father would find a way to take us to the zoo or take my sister and me skating. I saw how Mr. McAdams Senior behaved with his son at the office, and I could see how hard he had been with Greg. Maybe he hadn't had a happy childhood. But I didn't ask.

His eyes focused on the game, and a thought came to mind. I placed my plastic container at my feet, pulling out my notepad from my purse.

"What are you doing?"

"Writing some notes," I said.

"Okay ..." He stood up, his eyes going back to the court.

I got up and tapped him on the shoulder. "So, how do you play this game? Do you have to kick it in the net?" I wasn't ignorant when it came to playing basketball, but distracting Greg from watching the game was *way* more fun.

He looked at me like I had two heads.

"That's soccer. Have you been watching this game at all?" He chuckled.

"No. I've been looking up there, wondering how many people are in the stands," I said, looking around me.

When my eyes went back to Greg, his lips went thin.

"Okay, I'll give you a fast rundown, so pay attention." He leaned closer, enough that I could feel his warm breath on my ear.

"There are twelve active players, five players on the floor on each team. A player can dribble the ball, pass, or shoot. There's more to it, but I'll explain later, I want to watch the game." When he realized he'd lost my attention, he said, "What are you doing now?"

"I'm writing it down," I said, biting the side of my cheek to stop myself from smiling. "What's that?" I shouted over the sound of the horn blaring.

The crowd cheered.

"Game over." Greg sighed.

"Already? Just as I was getting into the game."

I smiled, and Greg's shoulders slumped. It was the look of a defeated man. It served him right. Maybe next time, he'd think twice about forcing us to spend more time together.

"A way to know if a man is into you is by his actions. Does he gush about you to his friends and family? If he can't shut up about you, then it's a big sign he's head over heels in love with you."

10 Signs to Know He's in Love
by Staci Cortés

6

GREG

I WAS MEETING my friend Jack at the Volary Bar in the Upper West Side. It was too fancy for my taste, but I guessed its extensive collection of mid-twentieth century whiskey and its panoramic view of the Manhattan skyline justified the price I paid to be a member. Inside, the decor imitated an up-to-date gentlemen's club. The dark mahogany bookcase contrasted with the cow-printed club chairs scattered around the room, adding a charming and cozy touch. I spotted Jack at the end of the bar, already nursing a glass of tawny-color alcohol.

We had been trying for weeks to get together, but with our busy lives, it made it difficult to carve time for each other. Luckily, men weren't like women. Jack and I could go months without seeing each other, and when we hung out, our relationship was rock solid. No dramas, no hard feelings. We just got each other, but I guessed you could say we had gone beyond the bro code requirement. We were brothers even though we didn't share the same gene pool or hadn't grown up under the same roof.

I met Jack back in college, but it felt like we'd known each other all our lives. We'd had a different upbringing. Jack wasn't a trust-fund baby like me. He had worked hard to get to where he was today—an attorney and partner at Brookman Farlow Turner Lit Law Firm, which I admired him for. He was lucky though. I was continually trying to prove my self-worth. People didn't see me; they saw dollars signs—the kind I had not earned.

But tonight, it wasn't about business or my father, and definitely not Staci Cortés.

"Hey." Jack tossed a nod in my direction.

"How are you holding up?" I asked, taking note of the dark circles under his eyes.

I'm no psychologist, but it took a man to understand another. Men converted one feeling into something else. I knew he'd been taking new clients when he shouldn't and drinking more than usual. This was a way he was coping with his grief.

A year ago, his godson, Luke, had died, and Jack had played a significant part in all of Luke's five short years. When Luke had first been diagnosed with leukemia, it had been a real blow, but Jack had been set to do everything possible to save him. Flying him all over the world, getting him the best doctors, but in the end, it hadn't been enough.

As a friend, I worried about him because Luke had been the only stable person in Jack's life.

"I have my good days and my bad days. I miss my godson terribly." He looked up from his glass and met my eyes.

I tried hard to think of something to say, but I've never experienced a loss like that. I could only imagine Jack's pain.

"I've said it before, and I'll repeat it. If there's anything you need, I'm here for you, man. Whenever you want to talk," I said.

"I know. Sorry I stood you up the other day."

He tapped me on the shoulder as I sat next to him at the bar.

"You said something came up. Was this something a woman?" I asked.

He flashed me a confirming grin.

"Come on, tell me. Who is she?" I said, relieved he had something else going on in his life besides work.

"Victoria Fairfax."

"As in Fairfax Developers Group?" I asked.

Everyone in Manhattan knew who the Fairfax family were. At some point, I had read their profile on *Forbes* magazine or seen their pictures in the *New York Times*.

"Yes, but her relationship with her family ... is not on the greatest terms."

"Huh, kind of like mine," I smirked. "So, are you seeing her? Dating?"

"Not exactly," he said before he took a sip from his glass. "I don't know ... Victoria is amazing, but she doesn't need someone like me in her life." When he finished his glass, he got the attention of the bartender and ordered another one.

"Why do you say that?" I frowned. "You think you have nothing of value to offer?"

What struck me about Jack was, behind his attorney persona, he became bold, sharp, uncompromising. He was this force that drove him to get anything he wanted—women, money. He won just about every case he took on. Whatever he desired, he went out and made it happen. But I'd known Jack long enough to know he wasn't what he appeared to be. Jack Turner was a good guy, and this unattractive version of himself was what every man wished to be. Ruthless, detached men didn't get hurt, but it closed us off to something extraordinary, and we learned that the hard way.

"Well, you know me better than anyone else. I'm committed to work. It's the only thing I'm good at."

"I think you're just scared, and your career makes a good cover-up," I said.

Jack sighed deeply, as if he had been contemplating what I'd just told him.

"I know. You're right."

"Of course I'm right." I grinned. "Can I ask you a question?"

"Are you going to psychoanalyze me all night? That mumbo jumbo might work with your readers, but not on me."

"Just go with it." I shot him a look. "Do you want a long-lasting relationship?"

"I ... think I do." Jack drawled, making an expression that made me think this revelation surprised even himself.

"Do you think you want that with Victoria?" I asked.

Jack diverted his eyes to the glass. "To tell you the truth, I might have made things complicated between us."

"What do you mean?"

"I messed up. I took Victoria's roommate out to an event last weekend."

"What? Why not take Victoria?" I frowned.

"Because I asked, but she turned me down, so I took out her friend instead."

Classic Jack. He couldn't take rejection.

"That's one way to burn a bridge." I winced. "How many times do I have to tell you—playing games only invites players?"

"I know. It was stupid of me," he said. "So, how do I fix this?"

"I don't know if you can. They're close friends, right?"

"Yeah, but nothing happened between us. But I guess I was so charming, now, she's developed feelings for me."

"Victoria?"

"No, Scarlett, her roommate."

"This is a whole other mess. I need backup." I pulled out my phone.

"What are you doing?"

"Getting a woman's perspective." I quickly texted Staci about the situation.

Staci: *He's toast. Tell him to forget about it. Women never go after a friend's crush.*

Me: *Even if she likes him?*

Staci: *Yep, we women have unwritten rules too, you know.*

Me: **Facepalm* Where can I find these rules? In* Starlet?

Staci: *Ha! I guess you don't have all the answers, McAdams.*

Me: *I never said I did. I have you. Why do you think I keep you around?*

Staci: *How did you get my number?*

Me: *I have it for safekeeping— your address, too! In case I find my car set on fire, I can direct the police to the culprit.*

Stacy: *Ha-ha. I didn't know you were so funny.*

Me: *There are a lot of things you don't know about me. What are you doing?*

I had thought of inviting her to join us since my membership did include a guest. Maybe seeing me in a non-work-related environment might make her view me in a new light. Three dots appeared before disappearing and reappearing.

Staci: *Good luck with your friend, but I have some grout to clean out.*

She'd caught on that I wanted to ask her to come out, so now, Staci was brushing me off. After our friendly date, I had thought she had opened up to the idea of us at least being friends. But I guessed not.

"Is everything okay?" Jack's eyebrows arched.

I placed my phone down on the bar before looking up. "Okay, this is what you're going to do. Tell her the truth. Be honest with Victoria. That's the only way you're going to win her respect. Women know when you're playing them, so to get something you want, you have to give something ... and when I say giving, I'm not talking about money or gifts," I said. "I'm talking about showing her you are willing to make time for her in your life. Make her see you're completely invested in making the relationship work. Show her you're a great guy."

"Okay, you're right. That's what I will do," he said. "Enough about my problems. I want to hear about yours." Jack's eyes smiled.

"I have no troubles." I snorted. We both knew my life was nowhere near perfect. "My dad wants me to take over Nast Publishing when he retires at the end of this year, but I don't know if I'm cut out for it."

"Why not?" he asked.

"Jamie is better at managing the company."

"I think you're selling yourself short, and deep down, you want to take over the company, but you're afraid you'll fail."

I shrugged. Jack had a point. I loved my writing career, but it was always a dream of mine to run my own magazine. I guessed I felt like I never earned it.

"How is your brother, Jamie? I haven't seen him in a while."

"He's doing good. He's putting an offer in on a vineyard in California."

"A vineyard? I didn't know Jamie was a wine drinker."

"He's not, I think it's because of a girl—don't ask. Anyway, he wanted to get out of New York. Jamie said something about wanting a slower pace of life."

"I can understand that," Jack said, taking another sip from his glass before giving me a side glance. "So, who is this Staci ... the one who got under your skin like a tick with Lyme disease?" He chuckled. "Is she the one you texted seconds ago?"

"Lyme disease? Don't remember saying that. I was probably having a bad day when you called." I frowned into my tumbler glass.

"She must be something else to get you all revved up like that."

"You have no idea. Staci Cortés hates my guts. I have no clue why ... but I can't stop fantasizing about kissing her." I shot him a look. "How do you do it?"

"Do what?"

"Act like nothing bothers you? Not let anyone in?" I asked.

"You just said it; it's an act. I let people see what I want them to see," Jack said. "I wish I could give you advice on how to grow a thicker skin. If it's about business or law, sure, but love? I don't understand a damn thing about it." Then, he smirked. "You're the love doctor. You should take your own advice."

"I thought I knew everything when it came to women, then Staci came along and taught me a good lesson."

"What's that?"

"I can't get every woman to like me."

"I always thought you weren't that charming." Jack chuckled. He called the bartender over, ordering two more drinks. "Now, you've found someone you have to work for. Isn't that what you wanted? To have someone to want you for you and not your money?"

"Nope, she's definitely not impressed with my financial situation."

"Well then, there's only one way to win the woman over."

"What's that?"

"Vulnerability." Jack held his glass up. "To the women who drive us nuts," he said, clicking his glass to mine before taking a swig.

> "I could have taken her out to an Italian restaurant, but I wanted to make the first date exciting and fun, so I invited her to a Knicks game. My date arrived ten minutes late. She was a stunner, so all was forgiven. After I made sure she was comfortable and seated, I waited ten minutes in line at the food court.
>
> When I got back, she told me she didn't eat hot dogs, and the soda wasn't diet. By the end of the night, she told me she had a lovely time, but I knew better. This wasn't her jive and I would have known this if I had taken the time to ask. Never assume, gentlemen.
>
> The best tip I can give you is to save yourself the trouble, fellas. If she's not a die-hard fan of any sports, then don't make the mistake I did. Take the time to check in and make sure you know what she likes.
>
> To my female readers, men will slay dragons for you, but please let it be after the game."

According to Staci and Greg
Date Diary: Learn from My Mistakes
by Greg McAdams

7

STACI

"YOU DID THAT ON PURPOSE?" Jackie asked, laughing when I read the article about our fake date at the Knicks game.

"Me? No, never." I batted my eyelashes. "I'll force Greg McAdams to take me off this assignment."

"By making him wish he were dead, huh?" Jackie's eyes looked over her heart-shaped reading glasses, making me feel like she was going to send me down to the principal's office.

"Or at least he'd never met me," I said, swiveling my chair around to look at her sitting on the edge of my desk.

"You know, you can kill him with kindness instead."

"Yeah, but where's the fun in that?" I said, and she gave me a look—*I'm not pleased with you.* "I know, I know. You're right. I should let bygones be bygones."

She tilted her head. "You never told me what happened between you two."

"It's nothing—something. Anyway, it happened a long time ago." I abruptly got up. "Did you bring a lunch?" I asked, hoping to change the subject. "Maybe we can eat at the park before we go shopping."

"Greg is not a bad guy," she said.

I knew she was right. Whatever had happened, I just wished Greg would acknowledge it. I wasn't even looking for an apology, because he seemed to have changed. I thought I'd moved away from it, but every time Greg was around, he seemed to affect me.

"The Knicks played an amazing game though." I sighed, closing my laptop. "Too bad I ruined it for him," I said, feeling the guilt lingering close to my heart. I had a good time, enjoyed getting to know Greg a little more, but I wasn't going to tell Jackie the truth. It would only fuel her obsession with getting Greg and me together.

"Are you ready to go shopping?" Jackie asked, grabbing her purse from under her desk.

"Always ready," I told her.

"WHAT ABOUT THIS ONE?" Jackie said as she held up a black sequined dress with a big bow sash around the waist. "Too glamorous, right?"

I wrinkle my nose. "Um, maybe something a little more toned down with fewer sequins."

"It's a masquerade party, and you work for *Starlet*. You should be heading to town in sparkles."

Jackie was helping me look for a dress to an event Nast Publishing was hosting in two months to raise money for the children's hospital.

"How do you feel about being auctioned off?" Jackie asked as we made our way through the rack at Barneys.

"I'll admit, when Kate first mentioned it, I thought it was a terrible idea."

Since *According to Staci and Greg* had gone live, Kate and Mr. McAdams Senior encouraged Greg and me to attend these events so we could be photographed together, like a superstar duo, which we weren't, but that was what the higher-ups were hoping we'd achieve. It was all about branding.

It was Kate who had come up with this fantastic idea of auctioning us off separately for this event.

"But, when she told me it was for a good cause, how could I refuse? It's just dinner ... probably with an old, rich man." I frowned.

"Who knows? Maybe you'll hit it off," she mused. "If he's old, at least he'll have money," she said jokingly.

I held up a dress with buttons in the front, but Jackie made a funny face.

"No, I could never marry for money."

"Money can't buy love." Jackie chirped.

"No, but it could buy you these shoes." I held up a pair of ankle-strap Walter de Silva stilettos. "Not bad, only a thousand two hundred, with the discount." I sighed. "I wish I could take you with me, I have a good home, too. You would have loved it there," I said to the shoes, placing them back down where I'd found them.

Jackie laughed. "What were we talking about?"

"Auction, money and men—I think." I walked around the display of shoes. "Anyways, I'm too set in my ways to have a man in my life. I can barely live with my sister and a roommate, never mind a man. Men, in general, complicate things."

"Um, speaking of complicating things ... how do you feel about Greg being auctioned off? I'm sure there will be a lot of rich, feisty women who would like to get their hands on Greg." She eyed me from the mirror. "Just saying, the man's smoking hot."

I loved her bluntness.

"Jackie!" I flashed her a wicked smile.

"What? I'm married, not dead. Besides, I was trying to see something in your face when I said it."

"What's that?" I frowned.

"Admit it. You find him attractive."

"So what? He has beautiful eyes, a sexy smile, a killer body, and a good sense of style. His shoes are legit; he's charming and funny. But why would I care?" I glanced up, continued to look at me inquisitively. "What?"

"Right. That's what a person with no feelings for another coworker—" She adjusted her glasses. "But too stubborn to admit it—would say."

"No way," I deadpanned.

"You guys have been spending much time together. I figured—"

"It's work-related, period." I took another dress and held it out in front of me. When Jackie shook her head, I placed it back where I'd found it. "To be honest, Nast Publishing is not paying me enough to subject myself to spending this amount of time with Greg McAdams."

"I've found it! You have to try on this one!" Jackie held up a velour halter dress. "It's forty percent off."

Minutes later, I opened the door to my changing room and walked out.

Jackie whistled. "Yup, that's the one."

I glanced one more time in the mirror before deciding. "The only thing I could hope for is I fetch a lot more money than Greg or that my date will be younger than his. Other than that, I don't care what Greg does or with whom he does it with."

"It will happen in that dress, that's for sure," she said.

I met her eyes in the mirror. "What's that look for?"

"I'm not buying it."

"The dress?"

"That you don't care about Greg," Jackie replied. "Or don't have feelings for him."

"No, I'm a cold fish." I waved her off. "I've been dead inside since 2017."

She snorts, then said, "Admit that it could be possible."

I looked at my watch. "Oh, damn it. We've got to get back to work."

Saved by the bell.

"If a man does things for you he doesn't want to like shop with you—girl, you'd better hold on to that man tight."

5 Signs to Know He's a Keeper
by Staci Cortés

8

STACI

THE NEXT DAY, I hopped inside Greg's car, directing him to drive us to the Middleton Resort and Spa. It was my turn to come up with our next simulated date. After Greg had given me carte blanche on anything I wanted to do, I'd found something he'd never done before.

"Come on, it will be fun," I said over my shoulder as we walked into a room with the sounds of rushing water and birds.

We sat in cushioned chairs, wearing matching white robes. Our feet were soaking in warm water while nail technicians buffed our fingernails. The walls were a beautiful ocean blue, with a few fake plants in the corners.

"Is this relaxing?" I asked softly. Turning to him, I saw his look of dismay.

"I can't believe you talked me into this," he said flatly.

"This is every woman's dream date. Trust me," I said. "They won't paint your nails any crazy colors, don't worry." I picked out a dark shade of red for myself. "After we get our massages, we can do something you want, but we need to loosen up first."

"We won't be massaging each other, will we?" His eyebrows joggled.

I rolled my eyes. "That's not how this works. Anyhow, my fingers are too delicate to be rubbing the knots out of your back," I said.

"Hey, I'm the most relaxed person in the world," he said. "You're the one who needs to loosen up."

I glanced at him. "I'm confident and opinionated. It's not my fault it intimidates you."

He scoffed. "You don't intimidate me. You're challenging, and I like that."

"Is that a compliment?"

"It is. If you were easy, I would have had you in bed at first sight of my motorcycle outfit." He grinned wolfishly.

The nail technicians exchanged strange looks while I laughed uncontrollably.

"You mean to tell me you have a specific motorcycle outfit?"

"I have several, depending on the woman. What's it to you?"

"So, which one did you choose for me?"

"The basic one. Not too flashy, but enticing enough to make you feel like you're living dangerously."

"You think you're dangerous?" I giggled.

"I have my moments," he said. "I was kidding, by the way. I don't have a specific outfit to get you to drool over me." He shot me a mischievous grin.

"Ha! Dream on." I turned away so he wouldn't see me blush.

AFTER WE GOT OUR MASSAGES, we returned outside into the fresh air, feeling rejuvenated. I looked at Greg. He was looking more stressed than when he'd come in. Funny, I didn't think I'd ever seen his hair so disheveled.

"Are you okay?"

"Are they supposed to be that rough?" he asked.

I tried hard not to laugh. "Yeah, of course," I said, sliding on my sunglasses. Maybe I shouldn't have said anything to the masseuse.

"You had something to do with it. What happened back there?"

"I don't know what you're talking about," I said, and he looked at me like he didn't buy it.

"Let's eat," Greg said, patting his stomach. "I'm starving."

"It's your day," I said, swinging my purse around. "Where do you want to go?"

"If you're buying, I want to go to the most expensive place in the city."

I grimaced, remembering my credit card payment was due. "Does it have to be the most expensive?"

"If you want to make it up to me, yes," he said, patting my back.

"Why don't we try the Chinese place we passed on the way here?" I asked as Greg held the door open for me. "It just opened. It's supposed to be extremely good." I slipped into his car.

Greg stared at me, stroking the five o'clock shadow on his chin. "I don't know, Staci. You said, after the massage, I could do what I wanted."

"Did I say that?" I shrugged.

"You're not a woman of your word, Miss Cortés."

"Please?" I jutted out my bottom lip.

"All right. How can I say no to a pretty face?"

"You can't. You're a man. You all have a common weakness."

"As do women," he shot back.

"What would that be?" I asked, over the revving engine of his Ferrari 365 Spyder.

"Charming men with good jobs!" he shouted before we sped off down the road.

When we got to the restaurant, we sat at a circular table in the corner, sitting on brown chairs. Yellow flowers in purple vases sat on each table and landscape photos hung on the tan walls. It was quiet, and the sizzling smell coming from the kitchen made my mouth fill with saliva. The lighting was dim, almost romantic, but I knew it wasn't a date. I tried to shake away the feelings stirring inside me, but I couldn't help myself. I tucked my hair behind my ear, leaning in closer as Greg told me about his travels through Brazil.

"It's a beautiful place," he said. "Sparkling water, luscious trees. I wish I could go back though. I went there on assignment once. Took my breath away."

"I'm almost jealous," I said, sipping my water. "You've been to so many places while I've confined myself to New York."

"It's never too late," he said, opening his menu. "We could go together; I could be your tour guide. Separate rooms, of course."

"For sure," I said, hiding my face behind my menu.

"Let me ask you a question," he said as I lowered the plastic food list.

"Only if you answer it, too," I said, staring at the image of the Kung Pao chicken on the page.

"If we didn't know each other from work, would you be interested in dating me now?"

My pulse picked up. *Should I lie?*

"I am attracted to you," I said, trying not to blush. "That has never been the issue. Looks and personality need to mesh for me to be interested in someone."

"So, you still don't like me?"

I shrugged, trying hard to hide my smile.

"I didn't like you for the first few weeks you worked for the company," he said. "You were prudish, but now, I know why. Definitely hot though. No doubt about that."

"Sorry," I said. "I didn't do it on purpose, getting cake on your designer shirt. Is that what you're talking about? Two years ago, when we first met at Christmas party?" I said, grimacing.

"That wasn't the first time we met," he said.

As I looked up from my menu, our gazes instantly connected. "What do you mean?"

There was a heat in his eyes that told me he was seeing me differently, too. "It was your first day at the magazine, maybe the second. You were rambling on the phone to your roommate about how nervous you were. I could tell you were almost in tears. I handed you a tissue, you thanked me and got off the elevator on the wrong floor."

I gasped. "Oh my God, I totally forgot about that day. I was a horrible wreck."

Greg reached over, placing his hand on mine. "When you're not a brat, I can see the good in you. I know that's cheesy, but I'm glad I've gotten to see the better side of you lately. I've had a lot of fun, except for the spa." He cracked his neck.

"Oh, you loved it." I grinned, then the waiter came over to take our orders.

When the meal was done, we walked onto the busy sidewalk, the backs of our hands brushing against each other.

"Thanks for paying," he said. "I think we're square now."

"I don't know," I said, inspecting the shimmer of my freshly painted nails. "Something still doesn't feel right," I said as we stopped in front of Greg's shiny car.

"I agree," he said, opening the door for me. "We need to go on a real date."

I laughed, but he didn't, looking at me with a serious expression.

I waited for him to do something, and then I laughed nervously. "You meant that?"

"Of course." He smiled. "I wouldn't joke about it. As much as you're a pain in the ass, I feel the chemistry between us. You've dialed back the anger, but we still have this back and forth that I love."

"I can keep being angry if you want. Annoying you is fun."

"See? Why not give it a try?"

"Because we work together, and I don't date people from work," I said, disappointed.

"Aren't you curious? I know there's a fire in you. I wouldn't want to stop that. Come out to a club with me—or better yet, I'll cook dinner for you at my house."

At that moment, I wanted to say yes.

"No, Greg, you're my boss's son. My boss," I said, diverting my eyes outside the passenger window to the crowd of people walking by. "I don't want everyone at work to talk."

"So what? That doesn't mean a thing to me."

I turned to meet his eyes. "It does to me. Please don't put me in this position where we date and you find out I'm not for you. Things are finally good between us. I don't want to ruin our friendship."

"Somebody must have done a real number on you." He nodded in defeat.

We drove off in silence, making our way back to work.

> **"** So, you took her on a couple of dates and got her to open up about herself. You think things are going well until she gives you the It's Not You, It's Me speech. How do you recover from that? Accept that you got rejected. Be the adult. You're not going to win her back by being needy or aggressive. Instead, treat her like a friend. Give her space, and it won't be long before she realizes she would have to work harder to win you back. **"**

How to Deal with Rejection
by Greg McAdams

9

STACI

"WHERE ARE YOU? We have to go over the next issue," I said with my phone between my ear and shoulder, my eyes catching Jackie across my desk.

It wasn't like Greg to miss a day of work.

"I'm taking the day off." Greg sounded odd.

"What's the matter with you?"

"I'm sick with a cold." He coughed, but it was coming across sounding forced and unnatural.

"All right," I sighed. "The new post goes out this Friday. I guess I will have to make the decisions without you." I tried to bait him, knowing the magazine was Greg's baby. There was no way he would give me full responsibility without having his input.

"I'm fully confident you can," he said.

He fully trusted me?

I had spent last night awake, thinking about us, wondering if I had made the right decision. I knew we'd had something going on between us from the first time we met. It didn't start at Nast Publishing, but at Pelham Country Club. The thing was, I knew he had changed, but my heart was not ready to leave things in the past. Maybe it never would be.

"Okay, get some rest. You should eat chicken soup."

Why did I say that? I guess I cared. We were friends if not anything else.

"Yeah ... okay, I've got to go," he said before the line goes dead.

It was not like Greg to miss a day of work.

I shut down my laptop then reached for my navy blazer, the one, every time I wear it, Greg calls me Popeye.

"Where are you going?" Jackie asked.

"Oh, I have some research to do." I threw my purse over my shoulder. "I'll be back in an hour."

"Sure. Does this research have something to do with Greg?" I hated it when Jackie saw right through me.

"No, of course not." I made my way to the door.

"Tell Greg I hope he feels better," Jackie said just before I walked out the door.

TWENTY MINUTES LATER, I arrived at Greg's apartment located in midtown Manhattan. I hoped to catch him at home and see what's really going on with him. When Greg opened the door, his eyes didn't look puffy or red around his nose—just like I suspected.

"Staci? What are you doing here?" he asked.

I noticed something else about Greg. He was bare-chested.

Jackie, if only you were here.

"How did you know where I lived?"

"I..." I composed myself, looking everywhere except at his perfectly toned body. "You're not the only one who can find things out." I cleared my throat and took the liberty to walk past him into his apartment. "Cute place, but I was expecting a penthouse with a view of Central Park."

I allowed my eyes the freedom to scope things out. Greg's apartment was cozy but clean, all decorated with neutral colors. Living area and dinette were in the same room, closed off to the off-white galley kitchen.

"Why did you think I lived in a penthouse?" He ran his hand through his hair and it caught my attention.

I preferred his hair better without the hair products. My eyes ran the length of him. So, this was what Greg McAdams looked like away from the office —dressed in a pair of heather gray sweatpants and nothing else. It was one of those situations that, once seen, it couldn't be unseen.

How am I going to face him at the office tomorrow without undressing him with my eyes?

I cleared my throat. "You drive a Ferrari," I deadpanned. "And a Harley."

"They're bribes."

"What?"

"Gifts from my father," he said.

"Is your father looking for any children to adopt?"

"Well, I think he's full in that department, but it won't be long before he's looking for wife number four. They do keep on getting younger ..."

"You wouldn't mind if I was in the running?" I winked.

"I don't want you anywhere near him. You're too good for him," he said.

My brows went up, but my eyes caught every curve on his biceps.

"Why aren't you dressed?" I said, holding out my hand up to his chest.

"Because I was hot. Am I making you feel uncomfortable?" He flashed a knowing smile.

"No." *You sure are.*

"I think I have a fever."

He walked closer and my hand went to his forehead, which felt cold to the touch.

"You seem okay," I said as our eyes met.

His hand goes to my waist, and I knew that look he was giving me.

"If I didn't know any better, I would say you're trying to kiss me." I arched a brow.

"I am." He smiled wickedly, waiting for me to move forward, but I forced myself to step back instead.

"Not a chance," I said, walking away from him, not wanting him to witness my beet red face.

"Not that I'm not happy to see you ... but why are you here?"

"I wanted to check out where you lived," I mused. "To see if your place was bigger than mine."

"Aha! That's the Staci I know." His crooked grin came out full force. "But, um ... not to see if I'm okay?"

I turned around to find him now stretched out on his white couch, his hair resting on top of his closed eyes. I had the urge to allow my hand to wander through his soft strands of hair and grip them tight ... only without malice.

Keep it together, Staci. This is Greg, the man you despise.

Only it didn't feel like that anymore. Maybe it wasn't a good idea to come over. It wasn't until now I realized how much more enthralled I was with Greg. It was an attraction and nothing else. Perfectly reasonable when you worked in close proximity with someone.

"Yeah. Whatever. That, too," I said, and Greg chuckled.

"Do you mind if I bring this into the kitchen?" I hold up the restaurant bag. "I brought you chicken soup. Want some?"

"Only if you will feed it to me." He smiled, and I had the urge to roll my eyes at him.

"Not a chance, McAdams. Not a chance."

In his kitchen, I grabbed two spoons from the drawer. When I turned, he was there behind me. So close I could feel the warmth of his body roll off him.

"So ... you're not really sick." I looked up and met his eyes.

"No."

"You didn't come to work today ... was it because of me? Because I turned you down yesterday?"

He lets out a long sigh. "No ... not everything I do revolves around you, Miss Cortés," he said without looking at me.

He took the two plastic bowls out of my hands, and I followed him out to the dining table.

"So, what is it then?" I asked. "I don't mean to pry into your life, but—"

"But you will anyway." He shot me one of his sexy smiles I loved to hate. "I'll tell you since you're nosy."

"I'm concerned," I said, handing him a spoon.

His fingers touched mine, sending butterflies to my stomach.

"Ah, you do care about me."

"I care about missing the deadline in four days. I need you back at the office." I sat in the empty chair in front of him.

"If you say so." He scooped up the hot soup, blowing on it. He sipped it before saying, "My father is retiring in a few months or so— he keeps changing his mind. I think he's waiting for me to take over Nast Publishing."

"And you don't want to?" I opened the lid, stirring the hot broth.

"It's complicated." He swung those blue eyes to mine. "I'm the oldest after my sisters, so it's always been assumed I would be the one to take it over, but then I always imagined myself doing something else," he said.

"Hold on ... oldest after your sisters? What are we in, 1785? Don't your sisters want to take over the company?"

"Jordyn has her own architecture firm and two kids, so she has her hands full. Skylar has shares in the company but has never shown interest in working there."

"So, what is it you want to do?"

"I'm trying to figure it out, but I know I don't want to be forced into something I'm not sure about either."

"Have you talked to your dad?"

"Yeah, that's what led to last night's dispute." He said.

"Well, personally, I would take it if my dad gave me a company."

"You think I'm some spoiled rich kid." He sat up straighter in his chair.

"No, I don't think that." I frowned.

"But you do. Deep down, everyone does."

"You know, Greg, I think you have a lot of issues, and you need to work them out with your father."

"I knew you wouldn't understand."

"You're right; make me."

"I feel inadequate," he blurted out. "You know my father brought in my younger brother, Jamie. Only, Jamie doesn't want to be a part of it either. So, now, it's between my sister, who's six, or me."

"You have a sister who's six?" Jeez, how many were there?

"Half-sister. My stepmother is only thirty-five." He sighed. "I know my father thinks I'm not cut out for this business."

"Because he had the intention of passing it to Jamie?"

He nodded. "What if he's right and I fail? I'll never live up to my father's standards. He is a huge success."

"You will be, too." I liked the way he looked at me. "I've seen your work ethic. I see how you treat people at the office. You don't look down at them— you treat them as your equal. You're quick with ideas, and in my opinion, you'll bring something fresh to the table." I paused, leaning against my chair. *Why hadn't I realized* it *sooner?* "Oh, now this all makes sense."

"What?"

"*According to Staci and Greg*—it's a test your father set you up on."

"If I succeed, then the company is all mine." He nodded, and my stomach turned.

"Wait, were you trying to sabotage the magazine? Is ... is that why you wanted me on this project? Knowing we would never get along? You hoped this magazine would be a complete flop so you could get back at your father for choosing Jamie over you—"

His forehead furrowed. "Well, no, that's not true—"

"Oh, and here I was, thinking you wanted my name next to yours because I was the best writer you had."

"You are the best we have," he said louder.

"I can't believe I let you do this to me again. Leading me on, only to shut me down again."

"What is it with you?" he said, sitting straight in his chair. "Here you are, acting all concerned about me ..." His face was twisted. "You want something from me too, don't you?"

"Oh, like what, Greg? To be your flavor of the month?"

"I hate that you always assume the worst of me. No, you're using me to build your portfolio. Don't you think I know you've been applying to other magazines? I thought we had something good going on here," Greg spat out.

"We do."

"You say we're friends, but I know something is eating at you. Tell me what I did to offend you."

"Remember I told you I worked at the country club long ago?" I asked.

"Yes."

"And I had a huge crush on this one guy."

"I remember."

"Well, he flirted with me when he used to come by. Then, one day, he offered to take me out to dinner after my shift." I wiped my mouth on the napkin. "But it never happened because, when I finished my shift, I found him in the parking lot, making out with a beautiful blonde. I never saw him again, not until I started working at *Starlet*, right across the hall from his magazine in the same building." I finally looked up, meeting his gaze. "I don't want to assume the worst in you, Greg, but I have a hard time letting go of the past."

At first, there was a moment of confusion before his expression changed to a sympathetic one.

"Cece. Everyone called you Cece at the club." His face turned pale. "I'm sorry. Truly, I am. I was an asshole back then. But I'm a different person now."

I shook my head, not able to meet Greg's eyes. Maybe I shouldn't have said anything. This was going to make working with Greg very awkward.

"Look at me, Staci." When my eyes met him, he continued, "You know I'm a different guy. The guy I am today would never have treated you that way. I was a mess. My parents had just gotten divorced. Hell, you don't need my whole life story. You didn't deserve that."

"It's fine," I said, wiping my tears. *Why am I crying?* "I have to go."

"Staci—"

"No, it's okay. Forget I said anything." I grabbed my purse before heading out the door without looking back.

> **If you feel he should apologize for hurting you, then ask for one. If he doesn't, then walk away. He's not worth another minute of your time.**

Stop Making Him Hurt You
by Staci Cortés

10

GREG

THE NEXT COUPLE OF DAYS, Staci avoided me. The only interaction I got from her was if it had to do with the magazine. When I talked about anything other than our next post, she brushed me off. I deserved it—and I didn't. She hadn't given me a chance to explain, to tell my side of the story—not that I thought it would change her view of me because, damn, first impressions stuck. However, I knew, somewhere inside that beautiful head of hers, Staci saw me for who I am, not the shallow jerk that didn't exist anymore. If only she knew I'd never meant to hurt her.

I was mature enough to understand where the pain and inse-curities were coming from— weight, and with men. It was the one reason I could think of why she puts on this hard-shell exterior, but I saw past that. The attraction you have with someone begins with the physical aspect, but once you get to know a person the way I had with Staci, the connection was unexplainable ... outweighing any physical attraction ever could. The more time I spent with her, I knew she was the one. No one else would ever do.

Sure, no two people could be the same, and every relationship has its trials, including platonic ones. Without excitement to work out our differences, it made it difficult to keep the relationship going. There was excitement in me, and I wondered if she had felt the same.

I couldn't focus on work. I missed Staci, her feistiness, the way she kept me on my toes, the way she drove me insane. Somehow, I couldn't get her out of my mind or my heart, and now I was afraid I lost her for good.

I caught Staci across the hall, wearing black pumps and a hip-hugging blue dress that accentuated her feisty Latin curves that I loved so much. She cast her eyes at me before getting into the elevator. I got up from my desk and made my way across to *Starlet*. If she wouldn't listen to me, then I'd get Jackie to talk to her.

I knew Jackie was a big fan of romances with happy endings. She carried one of those historical romance novels around the office like it was a Bible. If anyone could help me out, it was Jackie. Staci would listen to her. All I know was, I couldn't go down without a fight.

"Hey, Jackie."

"What happened between you two?" Jackie didn't miss a beat, typing away at her keyboard.

"Staci didn't tell you?" My brows creased.

"Oh, she did. Staci told me everything."

"You think I'm a jerk?" I placed my hands in my suit pant pockets.

"Tell me your side of the story. I'll let you know for sure." She abruptly stops tapping on her keyboard, casting me a look. "I don't judge before I get all the facts. It comes with years of being in the business."

I sighed, pulling a chair up to sit across from her desk. "It happened six years ago." I slide my phone that's been chiming with e-mails all morning into my jacket pocket. "I wish she would give me a chance to explain." I let out a long breath. "At the time, I really thought we had a connection, and that woman she caught me kissing was my ex-girlfriend, whom, at the time, made it her mission to get me back. What Staci didn't see was I pushed her away. I did go back inside to find her, only to learn she had already gone. I went back a week later, but her boss told me that she'd quit." I felt a pang at the bottom of my stomach, realizing she had because of me.

"I don't want to get involved between you two, but for a couple of people who are supposed to be experts in the dating department, you guys kind of suck at it." Her lips thinned out.

"You think you can talk to her? At least to convince her to give me a second to explain?"

"Look, Staci is not upset with you ... not even a bit. But she has insecurities. Why do you think Staci wears heels all the time? She thinks it makes her look tall and thinner. Also, when you kissed your ex—the one with the perfect body—how do you think it made her feel? She was much rounder back then. You remember that, right?"

"Yeah, but that wasn't ever the issue for me. Honestly, it's never been the issue. I love a woman with meat on them. More for me to hold on to," I smirked.

A smile tugged at her lips. "But something bothers me. All this time, you didn't recognize who Staci was?" she asked.

"Jackie, I was young. I had a terrible motorcycle accident two months after the fact. I don't remember every moment in my life. I'm sorry that she's hurt by it, but I'm not trying to play any games here."

"I like you, Greg McAdams. I see that you care for her. I really do." A look of understanding crossed her features. "But she thinks you'll hurt her, and she's been burned before—not only by you. Don't look surprised. She might have her moments of true hatred toward you, but you're not the reason she's a hot mess when it comes to relationships."

I glanced at Staci's empty chair. "Where did she go?"

"Staci is on a date."

"What? With whom?" I squared my shoulders.

"I thought that would get your attention." Jackie flashed me a smile. "She's working on an assignment that Kate wanted to do for *Starlet*. She's testing out the best dating app for her readers."

"So, she's meeting someone she's never met before?" The muscles of my jaw tightened.

"They've been texting each other. What's wrong, Greg? You look a little pale."

I cleared my throat. "Nothing is wrong. I'm concerned ... as a friend." *I'm such an idiot.*

"Sure, you are." She smiled.

"Where did you say she was meeting this guy?"

"I didn't, and Staci warned me not to tell you anything," She fluffed her hair then straightened her jacket when she got up from her chair, moving around me. "I feel like having a coffee. Would you like one?"

"No, thanks."

"And Greg, don't you dare go looking into Staci's day planner she purposely left on her desk." She winked before walking away.

"Remind me to promote you once I take over as CEO," I said before she got too far.

"I'll hold you to it," Jackie said.

I waited until Jackie was out of sight before moving out of my chair. I was thankful that Staci was still traditional when it came to organizing her schedule and that I didn't need the IT guy to override her password on her computer—I would if needed.

I sat in Staci's chair, opening her agenda to today's date. She was meeting a man named Matt at San Carlo restaurant in SoHo. I felt my whole inside burning. I got up and straightened my tie. What was I going to say or do? I guessed I would worry about it when I got there.

66 Be curious about him. Men love to talk about themselves. Just don't turn it into an interview. 99

7 Things Men Expect on a First Date
by Staci Cortés

11

STACI

I DISLIKED everything about online dating, and Kate, my boss, already knew that. But, if I were like one of my readers—a single girl looking for love in the big city—then dating apps seemed like the easy way to meet new people. Also, my readers would appreciate it if I scoped things out for them, though I hated the idea of choosing to meet up with someone based on their picture. If you met someone at a bar, face-to-face, at least you could get a vibe of what they were really like instead of making up this romantic idea about them from a profile picture and a few back-and-forth texts. Then again, I'd met Luis at a bar, and look where it had gotten me.

Really, I preferred a natural connection with someone when you least expected it.

Then, I thought about Greg.

Over the last few months, we had gotten close, and my feelings for him had evolved. I was not even mad anymore. It was silly now that I thought about it. People made mistakes, and people change. I shouldn't have treated Greg the way I had. But I had been broken one too many times that I didn't have the strength to go through it again—*trusting someone.*

Honestly, I was comfortable with my friendship with Greg, so I had to hold my feelings back from allowing myself to fall for him. The thing was, it might already be too late. I had to get him out of my system. That was why when Kate had proposed I investigate a new dating app that had just come out, I'd jumped at the opportunity. I needed something to get my mind off of Greg. Who knew? Maybe Matt and I would hit it off. Perhaps I'd be interested in seeing him again, outside of work. But Matt would never find that out.

As I entered the restaurant, my eyes caught a man sitting in the corner. Matt had said he'd be wearing a blue Oxford shirt. This man looked like the guy in the profile picture—the one of him leaning against a vintage roadster, dressed in a tweed jacket over a crisp shirt and jeans—only he was clean-shaven today.

I, being the journalist that I was, had taken the liberty the night before to learn everything about him, and thanks to social media, there was all kinds of information at my fingertips. First, I went over his profile, taking cues on all the information available. His bio seemed intriguing. He was thirty-four and owned a real estate firm. Then, I hopped on to Facebook and found his business page. I went through the recommendations.

One client wrote, *The most passionate and honest realtor you'll ever meet.*

Sounded promising.

Then, I moved on to his Instagram account. You could tell so much from somebody's life from the pictures they posted. Relieved he hadn't displayed much, I scrolled way down to the bottom, working my way up. He had a picture with a cute brunette, but it was dated five years ago. There was no evidence of her in his recent posts. Maybe a friend or now an ex. On a later post, Matt and another male were each sitting on a child's bicycle, which could mean he had children or a good sense of humor — or both. There were several pictures all over the world, including properties he was selling here in New York and LA. He had a picture of his dad and another post voicing his views on the extinction crisis of rhinos. Overall, I'd felt at ease, and I was excited about meeting Matthew Davis.

As I walked closer to the table, I had to remind myself this was for work. He was so incredibly handsome though.

"Matthew?" I smiled shyly, and he stood up.

"Staci?"

"Yes," I said, relieved it's him.

He offered his hand, and I accepted it.

"Please call me Matt." He had a charming smile, but nothing compared to Greg's. He was taller than I imagined and handsome than I'd initially thought, but something came over me. When I realized what it was, I felt a ping at the bottom of my stomach. He wasn't Greg.

"Thank you," I said as he pulled out my chair for me.

"Wow." His eyes held mine for a second. "From the picture, I knew you were beautiful, but I didn't know you were this stunning." He took his seat across from me.

"Thank you."

I blushed even though it was a comment I generally hated to get from men, but he didn't know me, and it was clear he was a little nervous.

"So, have you ever done this before? Used Heart Match to go on a date?" I picked up the menu off the white tablecloth, hating the fact that he didn't know the real reason I was here. Being deceitful sometimes came with the job as a writer.

"Yes. I have been on it for a week but have met no one interesting. I still have hope though," he said, and I smiled.

"So, what made you choose this app? If you don't mind me asking."

"No, not at all. With my business and traveling, I don't have time to meet people. The app makes things convenient. It's like looking at a menu, deciding what you want to have tonight," he said.

I wondered if I was the only date he had lined up this week.

"So, Matt, what is it you do?" I asked the question I already knew the answer to.

"I'm a real estate broker. I have an office here and in California."

"Oh, interesting." I slid a white napkin across my lap as the waiter poured wine into our glasses.

"I hope you don't mind. I ordered a bottle of merlot. I read on your profile that you're a wine lover."

"Oh, yes, that's fine. Thank you," I said, thinking it was a little too early for alcohol. I still had to go back to the office and deal with Greg. I needed my wits razor-sharp.

"You're a writer."

"Yes, for a women's magazine." I take a sip from my glass. I knew he was a smart man, maybe he might see right through me.

He continued to stare at me like he wanted to know more. "What kind of articles do you write?"

"Oh, um ... beauty products and fashion—stuff like that," I said, feeling awful about misleading him, but I was doing my job.

Later, we ordered our meals and chatted about the kind of food we liked to eat while he occasionally glanced up and smiled. Everything seemed to go great until I looked up and saw Greg from across the room. My heart dropped.

"Are you okay?" Matt asked.

"Yes ... fine," I said, choking on my wine. "It went down the wrong way."

I watched Greg talk to the hostess before his eyes met mine. He had a funny expression in his eyes. *Was that a look of hurt?* Before long, he made his way over to us. The heat in the back of my neck rose. I couldn't believe Jackie told him where I was.

"Staci!"

"Hi ... Greg." I wasn't sure if I should stand or stay seated. Either way, I had a feeling he would rat me out. "What are you doing here?" I asked through gritted teeth as he leaned in, kissing both cheeks. I felt my face stung. This small, intimate interaction was something he had never done before.

"I was just coming in for a bite," he said, turning his eyes from my date to look back at me. "What a surprise. I didn't expect to find you here," he added.

I narrowed my eyes and gave him my best counterfeit smile. I didn't buy any of it.

"I thought you would have your soggy sandwich in the lunch room?"

"I stopped doing that since this colleague of mine kept eating my sandwiches so she could get my attention. I think she has a huge crush on me." He smiled sheepishly.

"Oh, I doubt that. I think it's all in your head." I gave him a full-on glare.

"Do you mind if I join you guys?" Greg asked.

"Yes, I do—" I said, but Greg pulled a chair from another table, placing it between Matt and me.

"Sorry ... who are you?" Matt asked.

"I'm Greg McAdams, Staci's fiancé."

I couldn't believe he'd just said that. *What was he trying to prove?*

Greg held out his hand, but Matt ignored it. His mouth slightly opened, and his eyes went from me to Greg and back again.

"It's okay." Greg holds up his hand. "Staci and I have an

understanding. We are in an open relationship," Greg said. Matt's face went pale.

"Oh my God," I gasped. "Greg was kidding! He's not my fiancé." I shook my head in protest. I was trying hard to hold back my laughter, and at the same time, I had the urge to strangle Greg. "He's my annoying co-worker."

"Boss actually." He cast me a side glance. "Ah, man, I'm messing with you." Greg tapped him on the back.

Matt cleared his throat as he stood up. "I ... I should go."

"Don't leave. I wasn't going to stay long," Greg said in a tone that wasn't convincing.

"It seems you guys have some things to sort out. I'll leave you to it. Nice to meet you, Staci," he said, rushing to get away from us.

I didn't blame him.

"What? Why are you looking at me like that?" Greg switched seat with the one facing me.

"I can't believe you scared my date away." I folded my arms across my chest. "What am I supposed to do now? Kate wants the article by Friday," I huffed.

"I did you a favor." His eyes flashed back at the entrance. "Did you see what he was wearing? He had boring written all over him. You're welcome." His eyes met mine, and there was something playful in them, like he'd just won a tournament.

Did he think I was on a real date?

"You're proud of yourself," I said.

He leaned toward me. "I am. You deserve someone—"

"Like you?" I mumbled, knowing exactly where this conversation was going.

Greg was here because the thought of me being out with another man drove him crazy, and somehow, I enjoyed knowing that.

"It wouldn't be a bad idea." He held his hands out. "You could use someone like me in your life." He straightened his tie.

"You'd drive me crazy. We would end up killing each other," I said, lifting my chin.

"I don't think so."

"Says you." I snorted.

The waiter brought our lunch, and Greg now had Matt's meal in front of him.

"Jeez, is this guy for real?" He looked down at the Thai salad. "You know what this means."

"What?" I glanced up from my plate.

"The guy is a wimp."

"That's ridiculous," I scoffed.

"I mean, a guy doesn't have to order prime rib to prove to you that he's a man. Having a fit body is sexy. Ordering salad with dressing on the side isn't." He held one side of his plate up to show me.

"Matt is a marathon runner."

"I know. Did you see how fast he got out of here? He didn't even fight for you." He pointed with his fork toward the exit.

"Why would you?" I regretted the words as soon as they came out.

His playful eyes dimmed slightly, and I felt like I'd hit a nerve.

"I would go to hell and back for you, if given a chance," he said in a low rumble.

My heart picked up a beat. *What am I supposed to follow up with after that?*

"Anyway, it doesn't matter." I diverted my eyes back to my plate, trying to move off the topic that Greg and I would never be an item. "Matt was a good candidate. Now, I have to start all over again and look for somebody else."

"Ask me the questions." He motioned with his hand.

"What questions?"

"The ones you prepared for this date," he said, picking at his plate with his fork. "I'll pretend I'm Mr. Boring."

"How do you know this wasn't work-related?" I leaned back in my chair.

"It doesn't matter how I know."

"Jackie," I sighed. "This is not going to work. It's not fair to my readers when all my material is based on you."

"All your articles are based on me?"

"Do I have a choice? You're always around me," I huffed.

"Do you know how attractive you are when you get revved up like that?" He winked.

"You're insane," I said.

"I'm super chill. Come on, ask me the questions."

"Okay, but be truthful."

"I would never lie to you, Staci."

"Maybe, maybe not," I said. "Okay, how long ago was your last relationship?" *This should be interesting.*

"My last serious relationship was two years ago. I haven't wanted to be with anyone—that is, until a couple of months ago." His eyes met mine. "I blew it because I couldn't get her to trust me," he said.

I cast my eyes down to my tuna salad, pretending not to listen to the last part. My feelings for Greg was quite confusing. One minute, I wanted to strangle him and the next, desired to kiss him. The friction between us was undeniable, but I knew it wouldn't work in the long run, and I didn't want to get hurt again.

"Why did you break up with her?"

"She didn't want what I wanted."

"And that was?"

"Settling down—the house, the kids. Maybe a cat or a dog."

"Aren't you too young for that?"

"I'm twenty-nine. I have everything else. Those are the only things I'm missing."

"The one." I nodded, remembering what he'd told me about looking for his soulmate at the Knicks game.

"The one who gets me without having to explain myself, the one whom I'll miss like crazy when she's not around," he said.

"So, I guess I don't have to ask you my other question."

"What's that?"

"Are you looking for anything serious or just a hook-up?"

"Hook-up," he said, and I had the urge to smack him. "Were you really going to ask that question? Matt would have said that I'm sure, so add it to your notes for your article."

"Forget it. This is not going to work." I was too emotionally invested in Greg I wouldn't even know where to begin to write this piece for the magazine. "This is not the kind of articles I want to write about." I placed my fork down, taking a sip from my wine glass.

"Look, what we do for a living is subjective, right? I don't have all the answers for the men who read my articles. I'm just as lost about love as the next guy. So maybe that's why I write—to figure out something about love and maybe even about myself. However, sometimes, you meet a reader who puts everything into perspective." His eyes softened.

"What do you mean?"

Greg loosened his tie before meeting my eyes. "A few weeks ago, I got this e-mail from a reader saying he was a big fan, loved my articles, and he was hoping I could help him out. He was crushing on this girl, but he was stuck in the friend zone." He paused. "I thought, *great, I can help this guy,* so I asked him questions. He told me he was texting her for two months but had never seen her face-to-face because he leaves the house once a month with his caretaker."

"I don't understand." I frowned.

"This person was in a wheelchair. He can't do anything without help, except for talking, and he's in love with a girl who doesn't know his real situation and, um ..." Greg diverted his eyes away from me for a moment and they turned back to mine, there was a glossy look to them. "He's afraid that she won't find him attractive, and when she meets him for the first time, all she'll see is the amount of responsibility she would have to take on."

"Oh." My heart tightened.

"And I—I thought of all the times I'd felt sorry for myself and how they could never compare to what this guy was going through. I have nothing to complain about. He goes out once a month ... it left me in shambles. Really did," he said with a glaze in his eyes.

I'd never seen Greg so open, vulnerable, and at that moment, I wished I could reach over and kiss him. But I didn't.

"What did you do?"

"I couldn't promise him anything, but I set aside a whole day for him. We Skyped, and I suggested what he should do."

"Did he ever get the girl?"

He smiled. "He's working on it." Greg put his fork down and looked up at me. "Yeah, so maybe what we do at Nast Publishing might not feel as significant as changing the world, but sometimes, I get that opportunity where I can really help someone, and it restores my faith in what I do."

"I hope he gets the girl," I said.

"Me too."

I saw Greg in a new light, overshadowed by the fact that I now felt ashamed of myself, that I had let the past control me. This was not the man I remembered because Greg was a mature and caring man.

The waiter came around. "Do I put everything on one bill?"

"Yes, put it on mine. I'm picking up the check," I said to the waiter.

"No, it's on me. I ruined your date ... article. Whatever. It's the least I can do."

Greg waved the waiter toward him. As I watched Greg pay the bill, I chugged down the two-hundred-dollar wine that Matt had ordered.

Greg was so sexy. My heart grew ten times bigger.

"The best way to get people to stop asking if you're dating someone is to meet them with humor. Tell them you're in a fully-committed relationship with yourself."

How to Get People to Stop Asking If You're
Dating Anyone
by Staci Cortés

12

STACI

"ROSITA JUST GOT ENGAGED, and she's three years younger than you," my *abuela* said.

Yay! Another wedding.

First Rachel, now Rosita. I hoped my cousin Rosita didn't ask me to be one of her bridesmaids. I mean, I loved the girl, but there's only so many peach-colored dresses a woman can have in her wardrobe.

"I thought you should know, just in case you wanted to bring a date," she said, her eyes peering at me through her cat-shaped reading glasses. "A year should be enough time to find one, no?" Her red lips—the way they twitched on the sides made me think she wasn't done with me yet. As much as I love how my *abuela* throws out these offhand comments while sitting there, smiling so innocently, I decided it was best not to engage.

I knew what she was thinking—*the question*. The one I had been taunted with since Luis had broken up with me. The one I had been asked at every family occasion, dinner, wedding, and even at funerals. *Why are you single?* Followed up with, *How's that possible when you're a relationship columnist?*

It was ironic, I know, but being single didn't mean I was less qualified to do my job. Did chefs, after twelve-plus hours, go home and create masterful recipes? Probably not. It was the same for me. I wrote and thought about relationships for eight hours a day. The last thing on my mind is to want a relationship or fantasize about kissing Greg. Maybe it'd happened ... once or twice in an hour, but whatever, no biggie.

It was moments like these I wished I were a man. Life was more comfortable for a guy. They didn't get judged for being single. If you were a woman close to thirty with no prospects of marriage in sight, well, there was something wrong with you.

I hate double standards.

So my career, like my grandmother believed, was a man repeller because men didn't like an independent woman.

"I'm happy for her. I'll call Rosita later to congratulate her on the happy news," I said to my *abuela* sitting across from my parents' dinner table.

I felt my stomach twist. It was bad enough I would be dateless to my cousin Rachel's wedding that was coming up in less than a month. Now, I have a year's worth of torture coming my way.

"So, what are you waiting for?" my grandmother asked me in her Cuban accent.

"Well, I had my eye on the Prince of Wales, but he's married now, so I guess I'm stuck going to the wedding alone." I shrugged, watching my mother shift in her chair.

Oh, she's just itching to get into the action.

"It's not a joke, *mi hija*. What do you think you are? Benjamin Button?" My mother's eyes scanned my face. "Have you been using the Olay Anti-Aging I bought you?"

I knew they meant well, but this was ridiculous.

"You could use smoothing around your eyes," my *abuela*

chimed in, showing on her face where she thinks my problem areas were.

Apparently, my whole head.

I sighed. "Can I enjoy my dinner without talking about my skin or the fact no one wants to date me? But thanks for your concerns. I'm overjoyed with how things are in my life."

"Okay." My grandmother shook her shoulders. "Touchy, touchy."

The room went quiet not even a minute before my mother said, "Last night, I prayed for you, that you'd meet a nice man."

"For the love of God, Mom." I placed my fork down because I just lost my appetite.

"This morning, Margarita called me, and guess what? Her son, Edwardo, just broke up with his girlfriend. He's the perfect man for you, *mi hija,*" my mom said.

Oh, joy, here we go.

I give my sister, Elena, *the* look. The kind that said, *I wish our lovely mother wouldn't meddle in our love life.*

Since the age of twenty-two, my mother, Lydia, had taken it upon herself to find me a husband, and it was exhausting. I understood my mother was old-fashioned, but for heaven's sake, toss me a bone. This was not the eighteenth century, and I was still young, focusing on my career.

"No way." I shake my head. "Nope."

"*Como que no?* What do you mean, no?"

"Do you remember the last time you set me up with Carlos?" I asked.

"Carlos was a nice boy." She frowned. "You're too picky." She waved me off.

"He still lived with his parents," I deadpanned.

"That's because he's saving his money to buy a house."

"He's forty-five," I said.

"And soon, you will be, too!" She cast a look in my direction, and I glanced at my dad for support, but he had his head down, playing with his food in his plate.

"You can't start a family at forty."

"Why not?"

"*Por el amor de Dios*, because I will be dead by then." She placed her hand on her chest. "You're breaking my heart, *mi amor*. Honestly, after what I do for you girls, you owe me grandchildren," she proclaimed. I could hear the wheels turning in her head. "Unless ..."

"Unless what?" I said, looking up from my plate.

"You like cookies instead of Swiss rolls?"

"What?" I said, half-laughing.

"She thinks you're a Lebanese." My *abuela* shouted from across the table.

"I'm not a lesbian—not that there's anything wrong with that."

"What? You're not a lesbian—you choose to be single? You're going to be alone forever," she wails.

"Mother Mary, please forgive me. It's all my fault," she said into the air. "Where did I go wrong?" My mother turned to my dad. "This is your fault."

"How is this my fault?" He screwed up his face.

"You allowed her to watch reruns of *Murphy Brown* that glorified a career-minded spinster. What did you think would happen?"

"Mom, please." I felt a migraine coming on.

"Prepare yourself. You'll be thirty next year—"

"Twenty-seven," I corrected her.

"Doesn't matter. After thirty, everything changes—your hair, your skin, and gravity." With her hand, she demonstrated from her breasts down. "What kind of man is going to want that?" She diverted her gaze up to my father, who's sitting next to her. "Of course, I look good for my age, everything is natural, but who knows if you took after your father's side?" She made a funny face, nudging her head in my father's direction. "Prepare yourself because it happens fast. Start using the cream."

Please, Lord, make it end.

"I'm seeing someone," I blurted out without thinking—without knowing how I would follow up those words.

"Since when?" my mother asked. Now, everyone was hanging on my every word.

"I'm seeing someone at work." I started filling my mouth with food. "I didn't tell you because it's new," I mumbled.

"Is he Catholic?" my *abuela* asked.

I quickly thought about Greg. "Possibly."

"Oh, it's okay. We can convert him."

"Don't get excited. As I said, it's new," I said through chewing. I can't believe I just said that.

"Who is he?" Elena flashed a teasing smile, the kind that meant she didn't believe me.

Troublemaker.

"Oh, it's Greg."

My mother's eyes lit up as she clapped her hands together.

"Ah, well," I said, choking on my food.

"Of course. That's why you gave Greg our number. He wanted to get to know us, and you weren't ready to tell us of your relationship."

I reached over for my glass of water to soothe my throat. "What? Oh no ... it's not Greg."

"It is. You don't need to lie to me. I like Greg." She reached over the table to pat my hand. "Don't worry, *mi hija*. We won't judge you for dating your boss."

"I taught you well, *nina*," my *abuela* chants.

I love my family.

"Where are you going?" I asked.

"To call your Aunt Consuela and tell her to add plus-one to your response to Rachel's wedding."

"It might be too late," I said.

"For one more person? Nonsense." She waved me off.

"I'll have to talk it over with Greg. I'm not sure if he could take the time off."

"Okay, let me know as soon possible." My mother sat back down. "I can't wait to rub it in your aunt's face that Greg owns his own company."

I thought I would be sick. *Really, really* sick.

After a short second, my mother turned to my sister. "Elena, I have the perfect man for you."

"I'm a lesbian," she blurted out.

The whole table went silent.

"1. Fatten him up with compliments. A few compliments go a long way. Make him feel good about himself before you ask anything from him.

2. Go for the kill with a kiss. A guy can't resist saying no after a long, steamy kiss. We are women, and we know how to use our talents well, so put on some ChapStick and pucker up.

3. I scratch your back; you scratch mine. Pick up that cologne he likes or sees that action movie he keeps talking about. He's more likely to realize he wants to do something nice for you, too."

How to Get a Man to Do What You Want
by Staci Cortés

13

GREG

I WAS IN MY OFFICE, working, when Staci came rushing in, beads of sweat formed at her temple. She never came into my workspace, and I knew whatever it was, she meant business. When she shut the door, I straightened up in my chair.

"Are you here for some PDA? I like how your mind works, Miss Cortés, but I have a deadline to meet."

My lips went up at just the thought of tossing everything off my desk, kissing the life out of her. But then she elbowed me in the stomach, kicking me where the light didn't shine, and that was where my fantasy ended.

She rolls her eyes. "No, you insufferable man. I'm here ..." She cleared her throat and straightened her cardigan.

"Yes?" I watched her as her fiery eyes softened.

She casually strolled into the room. "Did you get a haircut?"

"No." I cast a suspicious glance up from my computer, catching Staci looking around the office.

"I like that shirt on you." Her eyes met mine as she ran her hand down her pencil skirt, which emphasized the curves of her hips. "Blue suits you," she said, tossing a strand of hair behind her shoulder.

Is she flirting with me?

I stopped typing and leaned back in my chair. "You're acting very ... odd." I allowed my eyes to take her in.

"I'm being nice." She frowned.

"Ah, that's what's wrong," I said, ignoring the fact that she tilted her head, shooting daggers from her eyes. "What do you want?" I said in a monotone. "Seriously, get on with it. I have stuff to do."

"I'm here to ask you for a favor," she said.

My hands froze over my keyboard. "Me, for a favor? You must be desperate." I chuckled as her hand went up to her temple, like she had a migraine.

"What's the matter?" I got up and met her around my desk.

"I did the most idiotic thing."

I guided her to my chair. "What's the matter? You look like you killed somebody." I chuckled.

"I wish ..."

Her liquid brown eyes looked up at me. I couldn't explain this unnerving feeling ... like I would go against my better judgment and do anything she asked of me. I just hoped it was not to bury somebody in Central Park.

"My mother has been trying to set me up with this guy."

"Who was the guy?" I felt the heat riding up my neck.

"That is not important." She waved me off. "I told her ... I'm seeing someone from work."

"Oh." I perked at the edge of my desk, looking down at her.

"For some crazy reason, she thinks it's you." She lets out a nervous giggle.

This was interesting.

"Really? Why would she think that?"

"Because she likes you!"

"Well, look at me. What's not to like? At least my charms work on some Cortés women. I'm flattered." I beamed.

"I should have never given you my parents' phone number." She let out a long breath.

"So, you came here to ask me what?" I straightened my tie and looked down at her. I had a feeling I knew what she would ask me.

"My cousin is getting married and ..."

"You want me to be your date?" I lifted off my desk, pacing slowly around the room. "I wish I could help, but ... I have plans." I met her eyes head-on. I had her where I wanted her.

The tables had finally turned, and now, if Staci wanted my help, she would need to grovel for it.

"But I didn't even tell you the date." She squared her shoulders off.

"It doesn't matter. I'm pretty much busy in the next few months." I paused in my step, sliding my hands in my pockets.

"Busy with what?" A crease formed above her eyebrows.

"I have to scrub the dirt off the grout of my kitchen tiles," I said, inspecting my nails.

"Ha-ha, very funny," she said, not looking amused. "I'll pay for your plane ticket." She twisted her fingers in her hands. "Did I tell you it was in Miami?"

"I don't need you to pay for my ticket, Staci."

"It's next week. I know it's last minute, but please, just this once, help me out? We could pick a fight at some point and break up. That way you can come back home early."

"I'm sorry, but I can't do it. It would mean I have to lie to your parents. I don't feel comfortable doing that," I said.

"Okay, fine. Name your price."

"Anything?"

"Anything," she replied.

How shall I play this?

Staci needed me, and there was no reason I shouldn't have fun with her after all she put me through.

"Wow, you'd rather deal with me instead of just telling your parents the truth?"

"Good grief. Stop being so righteous. Are you going to help me or not?"

"Okay, I know what I want from you."

"What's that?"

"A kiss." I brushed my index finger across my lips, and her eyes met mine. The way she was looking at me, I knew she had entertained the idea once or twice before. *I knew I had.*

"Here?"

"Why not?"

"But everyone will see us."

"So what?" I shrugged. "Since when does Staci Cortés care what other people think?"

"She doesn't—I mean, I don't." She abruptly jumped out of the chair and straightened her cardigan. "Fine, let's get this over with." She stood a couple of feet away from me. "What are you doing, standing there?"

"You come to me," I said, not moving a muscle.

"No, you come to me." She frowned.

Nothing turns me on like a strong woman, and Staci was that.

"Okay, then I wish you luck—"

Before I knew it, she was on me. One of her hands was in my hair— the other tugged hard at my tie, bringing me closer. The woman was an animal. I'd imagined this kiss would happen between us and would be great, but I never thought it would be mind-blowing. She forced herself to pull back.

"Are you okay?" I asked, seeing her flushed.

"Yeah, fine." She brushed her hair from her face. "Are you?" Her eyes dragged across my features, and I knew she had seen it, the heat rising inside me.

"Super. Great." *I hope we can do this again.*

"Do we have a deal, McAdams?"

"Just e-mail the details. I'll arrange everything," I said, going back to my chair, trying to chase how much more I wanted her out of my mind.

"Okay, I'll send it over later," she said, almost out of breath.

She walked out the door, leaving me there, wanting more.

" Do you want to impress a woman you care for? It's never the car you drive or the nice, expensive things you buy her. It's a man with integrity. There's nothing sexier than a man who lives by a set of values and standards. So, be honest with her. If you want a relationship, then say so. If you're not sure, then do what's right and let her go. **"**

How to Impress a Woman
by Greg McAdams

14

STACI

"REMIND me to thank your father for allowing us to use his plane," I said, looking out the window of the black Town Car that Greg had come in to pick me up that morning.

"No, this is mine," he said, scratching his temple.

My head snapped back at him. It's nice to see Greg out of his suit. I liked this look on him—a jersey V-neck white shirt worn with a pair of dark jeans.

"This is yours?" I asked with excitement. I'd never flown first class, let alone on a private jet.

"Yeah, once I take over the family business."

I noticed how shy he'd suddenly become, and I realized, in the time I spent around Greg, he never really flaunted his wealth around me. I liked him more for it.

The chauffeur opened the door, and I followed Greg up the stairs that led into a light-gray Challenger. Inside, Greg gave our bags to the stewardess while another one escorted us to the white leather chairs.

"This is insane. I should ask my boss for a raise." I winked, settling in the leather seat in front of him.

The interior was all wood lacquer paneling and trimmed in gold. The stewardess came to ask what I wanted to drink. I had an urge for champagne, but it was too early for that, so I asked for orange juice instead.

"So"—my eyes glanced all around me before meeting his eyes again—"you seem down to earth for someone who's about to inherit a jet plane."

"Yeah, well, I'll admit, it could get to me, and it had. I mean, I was born into this environment. I never had to worry about school tuition or pay my rent ... but money can become unattractive really quick."

"So, how did you get to this point?" I asked.

"Many things, but I didn't realize how self-absorbed I was until I had a terrible motorcycle accident that left me in an induced coma for a month."

"What? When you told me about the accident, I didn't know it was that serious." I leaned in closer.

"Oh, it was serious all right. When I woke up, I had to learn everything again—how to walk, talk."

"Wow. How come I didn't know this about you?"

"It's not something I like to talk about. I'm not proud of my life before the accident. I was a massive jerk ... as you know from firsthand experience. Who knows, if things were different that day at the country club, if I had taken you out like I wanted to ... maybe I wouldn't have needed the universe to teach me a good hard lesson," he said.

I felt the heat rise to my cheeks. Jackie had told me what Greg had disclosed about that day at the country club, the day I thought Greg had played me. Now that I think back, certain circumstances had kept us apart. If I had confronted him instead of running away, maybe things would be different for me, too. Perhaps I would never have met Luis. I wouldn't be so closed off to love. But here we were, coming full circle.

121

"I'm kind of glad we didn't hook up back then because I know I would have messed up at some point. You were way mature for me, and it took me some time to realize it doesn't matter how much money you have because it has nothing to do with how you feel when you wake up or how easily you sleep at night. Life boils down to having a roof over your head, food, and family. Sure, money can help with some of that, but it's never a shortcut to love and happiness. I still have to get in the back of the line, just like everyone else," he said, staring at me. "And what are you without love? A poor man in a designer suit." He shrugged.

"Is there anything else I could get you or your guest, Mr. McAdams?"

"Oh, I'm okay. Thank you," I said.

"Anyhow, I didn't bring you here to impress you. I thought, since this was at my disposal, we could use this time to get our story straight before meeting your family."

"Trust me; you don't impress me," I teased. "I still find you obnoxiously annoying."

He chuckled. "Not even a little?"

"Well, I could get used to this." I smiled as I took a sip of my freshly squeezed orange juice served in a champagne glass. "Look, I don't think I've thanked you for this weekend."

"No, you haven't."

"Well, thank you," I said.

Everything had felt strange between us since the kiss. It was like we opened Pandora's box. Now, neither one of us wanted to acknowledge the big elephant in the room.

"No problem. What are friends for?" He smiled. "So, was there anything I should know about your family?"

"Where do I start?" I looked up at the ceiling. "Well, my family can be overwhelming, so prepare yourself. Oh, another thing is, my grandmother is very handsy." I used jazz hands.

"What do you mean?"

"She has a soft spot for pretty boys like you. Whatever you do, don't turn your back to her, or you might get groped."

IN MIAMI, Greg pulled up to the waterfront estate, which was beautifully landscaped. I've always had a profound love for homes with terra cotta rooftops.

"Wow, big house."

"My aunt Consuela and her husband, Ron, are well off," I said, looking out the window. "We'll go inside and hang out for a little bit before heading off to the hotel, ok?" I said as the car pulled up in the semicircle driveway.

"Yes, darling."

When Greg shut the ignition, he got out of the car and came around to my side.

What a gentleman.

"Thank you," I said, getting out of the car. "For the love of God," I murmured, looking up at the house to find all the women in my family piled up at the front window.

"Are you okay?" Greg turned back to me.

"Yep. Uh-huh."

"You're sure? Because you look like you're about to get a root canal."

I let out a long breath. "I would choose a root canal over walking into that house any day."

He slid his hand in mine, making it feel so right. It made me wonder why I was trying so hard to put a wall between us.

"Oh, Staci, it's been too long," my Aunt Consuela said when she opened the oak doors, taking me into her arms.

"Aunt Consuela, this is"—I looked at the tall man beside me— "my boyfriend, Greg." When I said it, it didn't feel like a lie.

"Nice to meet you, Mrs. Ruiz," Greg said to my Aunt Consuela.

"Oh, thank you." She took the bouquet from Greg. "They're beautiful."

I liked the fact that Greg had taken initiative to win my family over. Even though the flowers were a nice touch, it really did feel sincere. It was not like Luis had ever thought about it when we came to visit my family.

"Greg, these are my cousins—Rosita, Clara, Eldora, Estela, Marina, Perla ... who am I missing?" I said, looking around the room.

"Me." My *abuela* appeared from around the corner with her hands in the air, all dressed to the nines, her jewelry on point. "It's great you're eating more, *mi amor*. Your face looks rounder." She patted my hand. "You were too skinny before."

"I'm the same weight as when you saw me last week," I said to my *abuela*. I couldn't please that woman. "*Abuela*, this is Greg, my boyfriend." Every time I said that word, it seemed like I was even fooling myself into believing it.

"Nice to meet you, Mrs. Ruiz. I've heard so much about you." Greg said to my abuela.

So he had. On our flight here, I had given him the rundown on everything my boyfriend should know about my family.

"Oh, nice to meet you." She took Greg into an embrace.

"*Lo que un hombre*," my *abuela* said while her hands roamed over Greg, making everyone giggle.

When she finally let go of Greg, she came over to me. "As in boy and friend, or just as in friends?" my *abuela* whispers in my ear.

"No— as in he's my chauffeur." I frowned. "But I told you I was bringing Greg—as my date to the wedding."

"I thought you were joking." She laughed then nudged me. "I am so happy you took my advice, *nieta*."

"What advice?"

"That cinnamon powder attracts men."

"Yes, *abuela*, I sprinkled it in my shoes every day." I smiled. "When I met Greg, he was instantly drawn to me."

"Never underestimate the cinnamon powder," she said, patting my head.

I loved my grandmother; she could never pick up on my sarcasm.

"Where is everyone else?" I asked my aunt while watching Greg charm the hell out of my family. My stomach twisted in knots because I had planned with Greg that, right after the wedding, we would have a big fight and break up.

"In the kitchen ... but where are your suitcases?" my aunt asked, glancing around me.

"Oh ..." I cast a look at Greg. "We're going to stay at a hotel."

"Nonsense. You'll stay with us."

"Thank you, but we don't want to impose," Greg, picked up on my signal, quickly added.

"You are insulting me now. Greg, get your suitcases, please. You guys can stay in one of the guest rooms upstairs."

"Oh, Aunt Consuela ... we don't stay in the same room. Also, you have a full house. We'll just be in your way."

"Why would you stay in different rooms?" *abuela* asked.

I saw it in her face; she suspected something. She's always onto me when I lied.

"We don't live together. Greg understands that I'm a Catholic girl and so—" I emphasized.

My aunt and grandmother simultaneously burst out laughing.

"You're so funny, *mi amor*. Do you think I was born yesterday? You have this," she said, pointing to Greg. "You expect me to believe you haven't climbed him yet?" she said, making me blush.

"Come, Greg, let me introduce you to the rest of the family," my aunt offers, looping her arm through Greg's.

I followed behind them into a large white kitchen where my mother and the remaining women in my family were cooking up a storm.

After Greg was brought out into the yard to meet the men in my family, my cousin Rachel leaned in.

"So, tell me more about your boyfriend," my cousin Rachel asked.

"What do you want to know?" I said, hoping she doesn't ask me something complicated.

"You will need this." My sister handed me a glass of wine.

"He drives a Mercedes." *abuela* smiled.

"It's a rental."

"He's rich?"

"So what?" I said.

If Greg were my boyfriend, money wouldn't be a good enough reason to be with him. It was Greg's big heart that attracted me. Always wanting to help people, and I had witnessed it at the office ... *even with me.*

"We don't talk about money," I said, and it was the truth.

"What do you do, Greg?" my aunt asked when they came through the patio door and into the kitchen.

"I'm a writer for *Avant-Garde.*"

"Ah, like my Staci ... but she doesn't drive a Mercedes," my *abuela* added for some measure.

"Well, technically, I work for my father," Greg replied.

"Ah." I could see my grandmother's wheels turning, and I wasn't sure if this information pleased her or not.

"You speak Spanish?"

"No, I wish I did." Greg gave her his charming smile.

"It's okay. You will learn." She tapped his face. "Do you want to get married in a justice of the peace or a Catholic church?"

My grandmother was only four feet tall, but she was very intimidating, especially when it came to her family. I guessed she had to be since my grandfather had died so long ago.

Greg looked over for support, beads of sweat formed at his forehead but the only thing I thought to mouthed behind my grandmother's back was—*Run.*

She leaned in closer, her eyes never leaving his. "In a church?" Greg uttered like he's unsure.

My *abuela* turned, and her face lit up with relief. "Tie this one to a chair, *nieta*, before he gets away."

Sure, I had rope and masking tape in the trunk for such occasions.

"Well, um ... we've never really talked about it, right, sweetheart?" Greg's eyes met mine. "Staci has been a real bright light in my life. I don't see my future with anyone but her. When the time comes, it will honor me if Staci would have me," he said, and my stomach thrilled.

But I knew he was saying this because I expected him, to—this was something a real boyfriend might say. So I wouldn't allow myself to swoon like the rest of them. I knew, by tomorrow morning, my *abuela* and my mother would have a list of people to invite to my wedding that wouldn't happen.

"Hopefully this will work out for you this time," my grandmother said to me.

"What do you mean? Did I miss something?" Greg asked.

"Staci was engaged before," my mother added.

I couldn't believe she brought that up now. Why not talk about my biggest heartbreak with Greg?

"No, I wasn't. We weren't engaged, not officially anyway. Never mind." I shot Greg a look and turned to my mom. "Can we talk about something else other than my failed relationship?" I said.

Greg stood next to me with questioning eyes. All I could do was shake my head, not wanting to get into it further.

"I feel useless. What can I do to help?" Greg asked my mother, who was in the process of cooking a Cuban dish.

"You want to help? Are you sure you want to do that?" I smiled.

"Sure. Why not? I used to help my grandmother in the kitchen," Greg said, rolling up his sleeves.

"Wash your hands. I'll show you what to do," my mother told Greg.

"Do you know who I saw at the supermarket yesterday?" my aunt said, chopping green bell peppers on a wooden cutting board.

"Who?" my mother asked.

"Dolores's daughter. She's looking like a turkey," my Aunt Consuela said as she motioned with her hands.

"*Tía*," I said. "That's not nice."

"I'm only telling the truth."

"Didn't she just get divorced?" my mother asked.

"Uh-huh. You can't expect to keep your husband when you wear your makeup like a clown," my aunt said.

Greg chuckled. "Are they always like this?"

"Yes," I sighed.

They switched to Spanish, which I'm relieved since Greg wouldn't understand a word of it. There was a lot of yelling and hand gestures.

"What are they saying?"

"For your safety, it's better you don't know." I told him.

" **The best time to tell someone you have feelings for them is when you believe you're capable of loving them honestly and properly.** "

When to Tell Someone You Love
Them
by Greg McAdams

15

GREG

AFTER DINNER, I went out and got our suitcases from the car, bringing them up to the room that Staci's aunt had assigned us on the second floor. We both stood there, looking at the double bed.

"I'll take the floor," I offered without hesitation.

"Are you sure?"

"Yes. Take the bed," I said.

She nodded, pulling her suitcase onto a chair in the corner. She'd been unusually quiet tonight, and I wondered if I'd done something to offend her.

A few moments of silence passed before I said, "You have an amazing family." When she looked up at me, I continued, "I would trade all the money in the world to have what you have."

She lets out a low laugh. "You're saying that to be nice."

"No, honestly. I'm the product of wife number two. All I ever knew was a workaholic father and a self-absorbed mother." I unzipped my suitcase to take out my small travel bag where I kept my toothbrush. "I have two sisters and a brother that I wish I were closer to and a six-year-old half-sibling that I barely know.

Tonight, sitting with your grandmother watching telenovelas ... it was nice," I said, watching her eyes gleam.

"Did she try to grab your butt?"

"Twice," I said as she giggled. "Nonetheless, when I'm around your family, it reminds me of what I never had. What you have here is gold."

Her eyes dragged across my face, and her features softened. I'd told her this not to get pity, but for her to realize that not all of us got the opportunity to come from a loving home.

"Thank you. I love my family. It's just they drive me crazy sometimes."

"That's what families are for." I smiled.

"Do you need to use the washroom?"

"Go ahead. I'll set up."

"I think there's an extra comforter in the closet," Staci said, and I nodded.

When she disappeared through the doorway, I found a striped, down-filled comforter inside the closet, laying it down beside the double bed. Then, I took one of the pairs of pillows on the bed and threw it on the floor.

Yanking off my V-neck, I changed into a pair of jogging pants. Staci appeared from the bathroom moments later, wearing the most unsexy pajamas I'd ever seen, buttoned all the way to the top. I felt like I was choking. *What is that? Reindeers? Who wears flannel pajamas in the summer?* If she's trying to repel me from wanting her, she's going to have to do something better than that.

"So, what do you want to do now?" she asked when I came back out from the bathroom to find her sitting at the edge of the bed.

Watching her, my brain went wild, but I was a gentleman, so I said, "I think I saw a board game in the closet. Feel up to a friendly game?"

"Yeah, sure. Why not?" Staci said before yawning.

"Okay, we have Pick-Up Sticks or Monopoly." I pulled down one box at a time.

"Pick-Up Sticks," she replied. "Monopoly is way too long, and I'm kind of worn out."

I turned, catching her staring. She diverted her eyes to the table at the corner.

"Want to set up over there?" she said, taking the wing chair on the left. "Get ready to lose, McAdams."

"What makes you think you'll win?"

"I have steady hands." She flicked a smile at me.

I loved it when she glowed. It reminded me of the girl I'd met at the country club all those years ago. I always thought she was beautiful and sweet. If only she knew it took everything out of me to ask her out that day because, around her, I felt vulnerable. Then, years later, when I first saw her in the lobby of Nast Publishing, I knew there was something familiar, but she'd changed so much physically and emotionally, I couldn't be sure if it was the same girl. However, she was there if you looked closely.

My one who got away.

"Okay, let's make this interesting." I watched her pile up the sticks.

She cast me an amusing look. "It's never boring with you." She snorted

"How about, every time one of us disturbs a stick, the other person has to ask a question, which the other player has to answer honestly? Are you game?"

"Sure. I'll go first." She grinned mischievously, scanning the sticks before choosing one. Staci carefully and successfully slid it out. "Ta-da!"

"You should have been a surgeon," I chuckled.

"Maybe I should have. I always wanted to be a nurse growing up. It was my backup plan if the writing gig never worked out." She giggled.

"Really?" The edge of my lips reached up to my ears.

"Get that thought out of your mind, McAdams." Her eyes blazed with amusement.

It was my turn. I picked the one at the far left, and just when I thought I had it under control, everything around it moved.

Staci leaned back in her chair. "You never told me why." She observed my every movement.

"Why what?"

"Why would you do this for me. Pretend to be my boyfriend? And I doubt it was only for a kiss." Staci brought her knee to her chin.

"Well, you have to admit, the kiss was pretty hot," I said, as she blushed. "I'm doing this for the same reason you came to my apartment bringing me soup. No one has ever done that for me."

"Not even your mother?" Her brows went up.

"My mother lives in California. I hadn't seen her since last Christmas," I said. Catching a questioning look on her face, I added, "I have a strained relationship with my soon-to-be stepfather."

"Oh ..."

"Anyway, I'm here because you needed me ... it felt nice," I said.

She looked at me like she wanted to say something but took her turn instead. This time, she was unsuccessful in retrieving the stick without disturbing the rest.

"My turn to ask a question."

"I know what you want to ask me."

"What's that?"

"About my ex—Luis?"

"Yep, sure. Only if you want to talk about it." I shrugged innocently.

She arched her brow. "You're kidding, right? McAdams, I

know you've been dying to ask me all day." She narrowed her eyes.

"You can't blame me for wanting to know. What's the big secret?"

She huffed before she said, "I met Luis at a bar, on a blind date. He was the brother of my cousin's best friend. He was tall, dark, and handsome. I thought he was *so* perfect. Boy, was I wrong." She threw the stick back in a pile before diverting her eyes out the window. I wished she knew how beautiful she was, so much I couldn't take my eyes off of her. "He was my best friend, and I thought we would be together forever. Then, one day, he left me. Apparently, he had another girlfriend in San Francisco," she murmured.

I cursed under my breath. "I'm sorry that happened to you," I said, relieved that I wasn't the one who messed Staci up.

"It sucks, you know. At the end of the relationship, end of that love, I felt like I had nothing."

She turned, and I got a glimpse of the pain in her eyes. I only wished I could take it away from her.

"Have you ever felt like that? Like your heart just burns?"

"Yes, I have." It was burning right now, but I could never say it out loud. It wouldn't be fair to put her in a position where she might not be ready to hear it—what I needed to tell her.

How much she meant to me.

"After Luis, I thought, *What's the point of love?* You're just going to crash and burn at some point."

"I don't think you really believe that." I played with the stick in my hand. "Maybe you're not approaching love the right way."

"Please don't give me any dating advice," she groaned.

"It's not your fault. None of us knows how to love the smart way..." I leaned in closer, close enough that I picked up the aroma of fresh soap lifting off her skin. She looks at me with those brown eyes and natural pink lips that kept appearing in my dreams.

134

"Greg?"

"Huh?"

"What were you going to say?" She hiked her brows.

I sat back, clearing my throat. "I let you in on something ... for me, I grew up with parents who never paid any attention to me. I was invisible—so lonely. There was so much pain in my past I couldn't think about it." I leaned in closer. "The only way I dealt with what I was feeling was by meeting a parade of women, but I was only re-creating the same mistakes time and time again. It wasn't love in the driver's seat. It was *distraction*. That was a hell of a lot more fun than sitting there, feeling sorry for myself, because I didn't know how to fix—me."

"And you did?"

"It took soul searching, but yes, the answer was inside of me all along. I needed to love myself before I could love anyone else. With Luis, you weren't the problem. He was too much of a coward to fix himself—unfortunately, you were only the casualty to his idiocies," I said.

She breathed in deeply. "Maybe you're right."

"I'm always right." I winked.

"The answer is not in someone else but inside myself. Hmm ... I like that. I'm not ready for love because I need to spend more time with me to fix the stuff that's stopping me from being happy."

"Well, that's not it exactly."

I'd steered this conversation way down in the left field when all I'd wanted was to talk about us.

"I can't be with anybody. I'm a wreck," she said.

"You're not a wreck," I said. She was missing the point. "Your dad said, growing up, you were more open ... the perfect child."

"I was," she chimed in. "I was overweight, which meant he didn't have to worry about me making out with bad boys in the back of their sports cars or whatever. I had a small group of friends, kept to myself, got good grades, and graduated with honors."

"Again with the self-deprecation," I said, shaking my head. "You need to stop that."

"With what?"

"I think you're being too hard on yourself with the weight thing."

"You asked."

"I did, but not to wallow," I said. "I want you to think about all the things you love about yourself. Trust me, there's a whole list I could compile on what I like about you. I want you to remember you're more than your weight. Though you do have some amazing curves." I flashed her a smile. "You have no idea how beautiful you are." The smile left my lips, and the air rushed out of my lungs.

We looked at each other for what seemed like an eternity, and if it weren't for a knock on the door that startled us both out of a trance, I would have kissed her.

"I hope I'm not interrupting." Consuela opened the door a crack at a time, almost afraid to witness something that I had imagined in my head a million times. Something hot and sexy—minus the reindeer flannel pajamas.

"No, no. Come in, *Tia*," Staci said.

"I wanted to bring you fresh towels if you wanted to take a shower."

"Thank you," I said, getting up, taking them out of her hands.

When Consuela closed the door behind her, I turned around to discover Staci sprawled out on the bed half asleep.

"Do you mind if we call it a night?" she mumbled. "I'm falling asleep with my eyes open."

"Not at all." I placed the folded towels in the chair I was sitting in a moment ago and turned off the lights. I made my way to the ground, placing my hands on the back of my head.

"Are you okay?" Staci murmured into the dark.

"Yeah, sure."

"Greg,"

"Yes,"

"It means so much to me that you're here." I felt overwhelmed, having her this close, like something heavy was pressing down on my chest.

"Hey ... Staci?" My eyes focused on a little light on the ceiling, coming from outside.

"Hmm?"

"There's something I wanted to tell you," I said, clearing my throat. "It's been bugging me for a while now ... and um ... these past few weeks, spending time with you, has made me realize a few things."

I waited for something ... but the room was silent except for heavy breathing.

"Staci ...Staci?"

I bobbed my head up to find her fast asleep. I stood up and brought the duvet closer to her shoulders and brushed her hair away from her face.

This attraction between us had become undeniable ... unbearable really.

"I'm in love with you, and I don't know what to do about it," I whispered into the darkness, knowing she never heard a thing.

"So you just ran into your ex at a party. Don't panic. You got this. The worst thing you can do is be rude or wear your emotions on your sleeve. It will only give him the upper hand. Instead, show him you're perfectly confident and that you've been holding your own without him. He will definitely feel he's the one who's been missing out all this time."

What to Do When You See Your
Ex in Public
by Staci Cortés

16

STACI

AS I WATCHED the happy couple dance under a white tent outside my Aunt Consuela's backyard, I couldn't help feeling a little envious of my cousin Rachel. She glowed with happiness, and I wondered if all brides had that allure about them on their wedding day. For the first time, I wanted that, too. To have someone in my life to look at me like I was the only one in the room.

"Here you go." Greg handed me a vodka cranberry in a tall glass.

"Thank you, darling," I said.

He was so handsome in his tux. I felt like last night, something had changed between us, as we'd connected on another level. It made sense, what Greg had said about how we used *distractions* to lead us away from what the true issue was. I'd chose to be with Luis because I couldn't deal with the fact that, being single, people would view me as unlovable or unworthy. And here I was, doing it again with Greg. *But what was I afraid of fixing? With myself? Was I using Greg as a scapegoat, or did I really have feelings for him?*

"Staci,"

"Yes?"

"I was just thinking how we survived these two days without you really hating my guts."

"I don't hate you, Greg."

I love you!

What was I supposed to do now? Greg was my boss. We had this good thing going on between us. I valued him as a person, as a friend ... but I sometimes wanted more.

Why was he looking at me like that? Like he wanted me to wrap my arms around him.

"I'm glad you said that because I wanted to talk to you about something—"

Greg's eyes were heavy like he wanted to tell me a big secret. Maybe being with my family was too much for him and he was ready to fake break up with me and go back home. This made me sad because these last few days with Greg were wonderful and I wasn't prepared to say goodbye to us just yet—even though our relationship had been entirely a fraud.

As I was about to tell Greg how I really felt about him, about us, I felt a nudge on my shoulder. When I turned around, there he was, someone I had hoped never to see again.

"Luis." My stomach dropped.

"Staci, it's been so long."

Not long enough.

Luis held out his arms, bringing me into an embrace.

"You look hot," Luis said.

I take a step back, running right into Greg's chest. Why was he standing so close? Greg's hands rested on the side of my arms, and for a moment, I felt relaxed. Luis looked over my shoulder, like he just saw Greg for the first time.

"Luis, this is my boyfriend, Greg."

The look on Greg's face was not something I had seen, not

even with my fake date with Matthew. It was more than being jealous. He was in protective mode.

"I hope you don't mind me complimenting your girlfriend, but Staci and I go way back. Our families have known each other for the longest time." He held out his hand to Greg, but Greg hesitated before taking it.

"Not at all," Greg said, holding on to Luis a little longer than he should. "As long as you keep your hands off of her." He smiled, but not the friendly kind.

Why was he making that face? He reminded me of a pit bull.

"Oh, Greg is such a joker." I laughed, patting Greg's chest. When that didn't work, I stepped on his foot, and automatically, he let go of Luis's hand.

"So, what have you been up to?" Luis asked.

I shot a look at Greg for him to behave.

"I'm still in New York, writing. I have a biweekly magazine I write for—*According to Staci and Greg*. Have you read it?"

"Of course I have. I'm not ashamed to say it, but I have been following you on social media." Luis smiled.

Standing there between the men made me realize something. Luis has no effect on me. Not one bit. No burning sensation, no hatred, just indifference.

"Oh, I see. So, you're *the* Greg," he said. "That's how you two met. I've read your articles for *Avant-Grade*. You're funny," Luis said.

"What about you? What have you been up to?" I asked out of politeness.

"I'm back in New York. I have my private clinic and work ten hours a week at the children's hospital."

"Oh, wow."

"You'll be at the fundraiser next month?" Luis asked.

Oh, joy.

"Yes, Greg and I will be there."

"I heard. Maybe I'll try my luck and win a date. You wouldn't mind, right, Greg?"

"It's for a good cause," was all Greg said, a permanent grin on his face.

"Well, I'll go and find your parents. I just had to see you first." Luis's eyes went back to Greg. "Well, it's nice to meet you, Greg."

"Likewise," Greg chuckled sarcastically.

"What's the matter with you?" I said, turning to him.

"What?"

"You're acting like a jealous boyfriend."

"I wanted to be convincing." Greg shrugged. "Anyway, the guy is a total jerk."

I threw my drink back and looked into the empty glass. "I think I need another one," I said, walking away.

" Be curious about him. Men love to talk about themselves. Just don't turn it into an interview. "

7 Things Men Expect on a First Date
by Staci Cortés

17

GREG

"MY GRANDDAUGHTER IS BEAUTIFUL," *abuela* said, standing beside me at the open bar.

"She takes my breath away," I said, looking down at Staci's grandmother, dressed in a long, elegant gown, her chin-length hair pinned up to one side.

"Can I get you something to drink?" I asked.

"Oh no, alcohol makes me bloated like a blowfish." She winked.

There was a moment of silence before she said, "I need to tell you. I have a problem,"

"With your bloating?" I frowned.

"No—with you, standing here like an *idiot* while another man is dancing with your woman," she said, holding out her hands to the crowd of people in front of us.

"What?" I looked up, scanning the crowd until my eyes find Staci and Luis sliding across the dance floor. Was that a smile on Staci's face?

My heart stopped.

"You have competition."

"I'm not worried," I said, looking down at my half-empty glass.

"Don't be so stupid," she said, and I chuckled, surprised by her bluntness. "Hasn't Gianna and Gael's story taught you nothing?" She batted her eyelashes.

Abuela was talking about the telenovela we had watched together the other day. When Gael had failed to tell Gianna how he felt about her, she moved to another country and married someone else. But I doubt this was the case. Staci hated Luis. After all, he broke her heart. *She would never go back to him ... would she?*

"You will lose her if you don't tell her the truth about how you feel," her *abuela* said. I snapped my head to meet her eyes. "You're the only thing close to making her happy."

"Why close?" I chuckled.

"Men always fall short in making a woman joyous ... when they get the girl, they get lazy with love, and sometimes they die, *eh?*" she raised her shoulders.

Staci always felt like she was out of my reach. I don't know if I could make Staci happy, but I would give it all I got trying.

"Staci already knows how I feel about her," I said, taking a sip from my glass.

"Stop the charade." She motions with her hands. "You are not Staci's boyfriend."

My eyes find Staci in the crowd, and when she turned, our eyes meet.

Does she want me to save her from Luis?

"Of course I am," I chuckled, straighten my shoulders.

Abuela gave me a look as if she knew better.

"Listen to me." With her hand, she motions me to come closer, and I hunch down. "Staci is stubborn as a mule," she said. "It's not entirely her fault. She gets that from her *abuelo*, God rest his soul." Her eyes brushed the ceiling.

"I know you American boys are afraid to show your emotions, but in our culture, there's only one way to win a woman. You must show her you *want* her—you *need* her. Be a man and tell her now, or else you'll lose her forever."

"You're such a smart and beautiful woman," I said.

"For sure. Where do you think Staci gets her looks and brains? She got them from me," she said, pointing to her chest with her pointer finger.

"I'll tell her tonight."

"Good." She smiled. "Greg, what do you think about these shoes?" she said, holding the hem slightly up.

"They're ... very nice," I said. *What do I know about shoes?*

"They're more than just nice," she said in a rich, heavy accent. "If you hurt my Staci, I know how to use them, okay?" She slapped my face harder than expected. "Okay, okay, we're good," she said, walking away as I stood there rubbing my face.

SLOW MUSIC CAME ON, and I caught Staci in a crowd of women. When I got close enough, I took her hand in mine and dragged her up against my body. Her wavy hair tousled around her bare shoulders. She was by far the most beautiful woman I'd ever seen. Not only because of her attributes, but because at that moment, I realized she was everything I had been looking for—everything I ever needed. All I wanted was to be hers.

"Dance with me," I whispered in her ear.

"Greg, my feet are tired," Staci groaned.

"They weren't tired when you were dancing with Enrique."

A slow smile appeared on her face. "You're right. Luis looks like Enrique Iglesias."

She turned away from me to search the crowd, but I motioned her chin back, so she had no choice but to look at me.

Only me.

"Dance with me."

She searched my face. "Greg, I'm really exhausted."

"I think you're scared," I said, sensing there was something off about her tonight.

Staci looked up, biting her lip like she was stopping herself from telling me something. Maybe she wanted things to go as planned—make a scene so we break up by the end of the night. I didn't want to take no for an answer again, so I pulled her to the center of the dance floor, and when we do, her arms go around my neck. Even though other couples surrounded us, Staci had a way of making me feel like we were the only two in the room.

I was in love with this girl.

"You must be excited to go back home tomorrow?" she asked, her voice hinting at a hint of disappointment.

She flashed her liquid brown eyes, and I melted. *Abuela* was right; I needed to be honest with my emotions, but I didn't know how to begin. I was never taught or shown. Every woman I'd ever met wanted something from me—a designer purse, a tennis bracelet, a trip to Bora Bora. I'd reluctantly given it because I didn't know how else to keep someone from leaving. Now, I realized none of it was ever real. You couldn't buy love—you had to earn it. Here I was, trying to win my way into Staci's life, to gain her trust.

On this trip, everything became clear. There was this new desire in me, to wake up every morning with her by my side. There was nothing more I ever wanted than what I had right here in front of me.

"I wish we didn't have to go back."

Her whole face lit up. "You want to stay here?"

"What I want is more time with you."

"I don't understand." She squeezed her eyes shut before opening them again.

"Come on, Staci. You know what's going on between us. I'm falling for you—fast and hard. I don't want to go back home if it means no more of this. I like being close to you."

"Greg—"

"Wait, let me finish. Years ago, I messed up the one opportunity I had with you. I was too young and immature to realize what an amazing girl you were," I said, out of breath. "I let you slip away once. I won't do it again."

"I hope you don't," she said, her eyes dragged across my face. "You've never been nervous around me before."

Had she been so clueless to realize what kind of effect she had on me? "I'm at the point in my life where I need something more serious, committed."

"Is this your way of telling me you don't want to be my fake boyfriend anymore?" She smiled, and my heart skipped a beat.

"That's right. I want this for real. You and me day after day."

"I don't get it," she said, shaking her head. "I was so cruel to you, and yet you want to date me?"

"Are you saying you don't want to be with me?" My arms pulled her closer.

"I do," she said, smiling. "I just don't understand why you're interested in me. I'm still confused about your attraction."

"You seem to think I've only noticed you when you're sniping remarks at me or eating my lunches—which by the way, you owe me a muffin." I grinned. "But I know, even though you hide behind walls, you care about Jackie, and you hang out with her kids when she has to bring them to work. You're focused and dedicated to the job, but you also make time for others. I only wish you would give me the chance to be a part of your life."

"Are you stalking me or something?" she said, tucking her hair behind her ear, avoiding eye contact. "How could you know all that?"

"I'm a trained journalist," I said proudly. "I can't help

noticing things about you. Our office walls are made of glass. My desk looks right out to yours."

She scrunched her brows. "Not really."

I shrugged. "Okay, I might have exaggerated that part. My buddy's desk looks out to yours, and I'm there, talking to him, sometimes. I'm going to stop talking now. I'm such a weirdo," I said.

"It's sweet you've noticed all these things. It's just shocking. I would never have expected something like this. Weeks ago, we were almost mortal enemies."

"I never saw it that way," I said. "I liked you the moment we met. See, the thing is, you're the first woman who's put me in my place. With you, I need to earn your trust and love. Nothing worth having comes easy."

"So, it's the chase you like?" She paused. "Once you get what you want, you'll just disregard me?"

"No. I don't see the point in playing games. I don't need to pull the wool over your eyes because you've known me for a while now. I'm not sure how you feel about me, but I'm not afraid to find out. Are you?"

"Afraid?" She laughed nervously. "No."

I leaned in, claiming her soft lips with mine. I kissed her in a way that made her understand I was hers.

"When we get back to New York, we should go on a real date."

She smiled. "I would like that."

Could this be real?

"Yes!" I pumped my fist in the air. "You're buying, right?" I said, and we both laughed.

"The most dangerous part of the relationship is the beginning—when you feel completely crazy about each other and you want to spend all your time with them. The consequence of that is less time with other things in your life that are just as important, like friends or your hobbies like shoe shopping. You need to slow things down and don't lose sight of yourself."

Are You Moving Too Fast?
by Staci Cortés

18

STACI

OVER THE NEXT WEEK, my life was blissful. The magazine was creating tons of buzz, thanks to our hard work and several sleepless nights to meet the deadlines. *According to Staci and Greg* was growing a substantial readership, and I knew I couldn't have done it without Greg's collaboration. I thought about how well we go together. After all, if we had a job in any other industry, it might not have worked between us romantically. Greg and I were writers and knew how much our careers demanded from us.

We were a perfect fit.

One night, I sat on Greg's couch in an oversized sweater that belonged to him, holding my laptop, while Greg went to get us wine, only wearing shorts. I could get used to this view, watching his backside as he headed toward the kitchen. Greg had an athletic body—not overly built, but there was more to Greg that I liked. It was the way he made me feel when I was around him— safe, loved. Even though we hadn't said those words out loud, we knew what we meant to each other.

That night, we had planned to discuss the magazine, but we

couldn't keep our hands off each other. I hoped that would never change. When Greg walked back, he took my laptop, placing it on the coffee table next to the wine glasses. Then, he pulled me into his lap and passionately kissed me.

"You are the sexiest woman I've ever been with."

"Oh, really?" I frowned as Greg nuzzled my neck. "How many women have you been with?"

Greg blushed and tried to look away, but I grabbed his chin, pulling it back.

"Come on, give me a number."

"Why do you need to know?" he asked, looking out the window ahead of us with a view of the city.

"Just because. Ten? Fifty? I promise I won't get jealous."

"Fifty! What kind of guy do you think I am?" Greg kissed me, avoiding telling me anything at all, and I pushed him away.

"Spill it," I said. "What's your number?"

"I'll tell you mine if you tell me yours."

"You already know I was a full virgin until college. I've been with two guys, plus you."

"That I was serious crazy about? Only you," he said as I gave him a flat look. "Maybe ten women—all flings."

"Ten?" I sat up straight and hopped off his lap, stretching out on my back across the couch, with my head resting in Greg's lap. He traced circles around my face, and it was putting me into a trance.

"With the way you talk to the guys at the office, I thought it'd be a thousand."

Greg shrugged. "What can I say? We're idiots. It's an act. Every new story is more embellished than the last."

"What about that girl at the bar?"

"We never slept together. I just used the barmaid to get your attention."

I sat up, kicking my legs. "You were trying to make me jealous?"

"You think I didn't notice you shooting daggers through my skull all night at the bar?" He chuckled. "I wanted to gauge your reaction. If you weren't jealous, you wouldn't care so much."

"I thought you weren't the type to play games," I said while he played with my hair.

"I'm not. It was just that one time to assess the situation." He grinned, scooping me up in his arms. "Does it all matter now? All my life, I have been looking for you."

Staring at each other, we smiled. "I never expected this to happen," I said.

"It can happen a third time tonight," he whispered, biting my earlobe.

"As tempting as that sounds," I said, jumping off him, "we have work to do."

I tried to walk back to the kitchen, but he tugged me back for a kiss.

"Why don't you stay the night? We can spend the weekend together."

"You want to be with me for the entire weekend?" I asked, placing my hands on his chest. "Don't we already spend enough time together at work?"

I'm surprised he isn't bored with me.

"It'll never be enough," he said. "Being with you makes my life much more thrilling. Why would I leave that behind?" Greg said.

I couldn't believe those words coming out of his mouth. Luis never wanted me to stay over, not even on weekends. But Greg was nothing like Luis—Greg was in a league of his own.

"Okay." I grinned. "How can I say no to that?"

"By the way, I finished a draft of our next post. Want to take a look?"

"Of course I'll read it," I said.

"I think we need a shower first though."

"You go ahead without me. I'm going to read your article." I smiled, getting out of his grip.

"You're no fun," he said, dragging his feet into his bedroom as I followed.

Later in his room, I lay on my stomach with his computer at the foot of the bed. While I was reading his article, his computer kept dinging with e-mails, interrupting my focus.

"How do I turn down the volume on this thing?" I called out.

"The volume key is broken. Would you mind reading the first few e-mails and telling me if anything is interesting? I haven't checked it today, but I don't want to be tempted to start answering them. Once I do, I'll be on it all night." His loud voice came out of the bathroom.

I opened his e-mail application and scrolled down the menu. The first message that caught my eye had the subject line *Congratulations*.

What was that about?

I turned my head to see the door was half open, and Greg was still in the shower. I thought it would be a while before he came walking out. It wasn't like I would be caught snooping because I was doing what he asked me to. Without another thought, I clicked on it and read it in my head.

Dear Greg McAdams,

The team and I have been impressed with your background and your extensive knowledge that is shown in your editorial piece, The South American, that you submitted to us. It was beautifully written, and I would like to further discuss your future with us at the New York Times. We feel that your skills and background will be an asset to our team. Please contact my assistant Kelsey Phillips, and she will answer any questions you might have.

The team and I look forward to working with you soon.

Angela Crawford,
Editor-in-chief

I SHUT THE LAPTOP. Did my eyes read that right? I swallowed hard as I shuffled down to the edge of the bed, watching Greg getting out of the bathroom.

"Is everything all right?" he asked, wearing a bath towel around his waist while wiping his hair with a hand towel. "Anything good?"

I shook my head, knowing if I spoke, my tears would fall. Greg moved to the end of the bed, putting his arm around me. He kissed my cheek, and I shrugged him away.

"Staci?"

Standing, I picked my jeans up off the floor. "I can't believe you," I said, struggling to put my pants on. How could he do that? Go behind my back and applied for the same position I was aiming for, without even discussing it with me first. What about what we built together, didn't that mean anything? Not me or the magazine? That back-stabbing son of—*gah*—*what's the matter with these pants?*

One leg at a time, Staci.

"What's gotten into you?" he chuckled when I finally put my jeans on the right way, and the fact that I was amusing him infuriated me.

"Are you upset with me?" he grabbed my shoulders, turning me toward him.

I stared at the ground. "Remember how I told you I was thinking about submitting a piece to the *New York Times*?"

"Yeah?"

I slightly looked up to see the thin line of his lips. "I think I'm going to," I said, hoping he would notice the daggers I was shooting at him through my eyes.

"Why not. I've always said you should," Greg said, seemingly unaffected by my mention of the magazine.

"Do you think you'll submit something, too?"

Come out and say it, Greg!

"I've submitted some short pieces to a few other magazines, but not the *Times*. My buddies think I should give them my South America piece, but I'm not sure yet."

What a piece of work!

I stood there motionless, allowing his lies pierced through my body, making my stomach clench. I couldn't believe he was lying to me. Why wouldn't he tell me he applied for the job?

"I'm not feeling well. Could you take me home?"

He hugged me and kissed my head. "You do feel a little warm. Why don't I make you soup or something? Stay here tonight, no use going all the way to your apartment."

"I want to go." I pushed him away.

I went to the bathroom to freshen up before he noticed that I was upset, but didn't I want him to know how he betrayed me. I leaned over the sink, splashing cold water on my face, as he knocked on the door.

"What can I do to make you feel better?" he said when I opened the door to the bathroom.

"I need to be alone," I said, walking past him.

"What's this about?" He scrunched his brows, leaning forward for a kiss, but I pulled back. "Can you stop trying to kiss me? Can't you see I'm upset." I held up my hands.

"Staci? What did I miss? Do you not believe me about the women? I've been up front with you this whole time. I promise."

I scoffed, wiping tears away. "I have to go. I'll call you."

Maybe. Depending on how I felt when I woke up weeks from now, cradling an empty bottle of Merlot.

I exited the bedroom with Greg following me down the hall and to the kitchen, where I grabbed my purse. I stopped at the front door, slowly opening it.

"Can you wait? I'll drive you. Just give me a minute to put some clothes on."

Looking over my shoulder, I said, "I'll take a cab."

"What is your problem?"

Seriously, I just wanted to be done. I wanted to stop allowing men into my life only to have my heart broken. The worst part of all, I thought Greg was different. How could I have been so wrong?

"I saw the e-mail from the *New York Times*, congratulating you on your article," I said. "Well, *congratulations!*"

He looked up at me with wide eyes, then his lips parted, but nothing came from his mouth. I've never seen Greg McAdams speechless, and my heart broke.

"You've got some nerve, lying to me about your new offer. You said you wouldn't hide things from me, yet you went behind my back—applied for the same job I was after."

"Staci, you don't understand."

"I bet you got close to me because you saw me as a threat. You wanted to swoop in, knocking me off my game, so you could take what I always wanted. You took an interest in my family and you got a good story out of it. That was clever, but I've caught on to your games."

"Can you let me explain?"

"No. I will not be a puppet to further your career."

"Hold on. I didn't apply for the job. They came looking for

me." He paused. "And you know what? You used me as a puppet, too! Someone to test your theory out on ... all those articles you wrote for *According to Staci* was about me!"

"I was doing my job." I said, making my way to the door.

"Oh, and you did." He ran his hands in his damp hair. "You're looking for every reason to put a wedge between us. I don't understand it. How do I know you're not using me to get ahead at Nast Publishing?"

"What?" I spun back around to face Greg. "You think I'm using you? I work my ass off, and you know that more than anyone. I don't need you or your company. I'm done with you—Personally, and professionally." I rushed to the door, letting it slam on my way out.

" If you decide to spend the night at his place, never leave stuff at his house, especially early on in a relationship. Not your lipstick or your favorite sweater, hoping it will give him a reason to see you again. You want him to want to see you— just because he does. So the only thing you should leave behind is the scent of your fragrance on his pillow so that he will remember you. Scent is a pylon to emotions. **"**

Three Mistakes When You Spend the
Night
by Staci Cortés

19

STACI

ON SUNDAY, Jackie called and I told her what happened between Greg and me. It didn't take long before she showed up at my apartment with a bucket of chocolate ice cream and a coupon to her favorite shoe outlet store on Staten Island. When I opened the door, the first thing she did was pull me into an embrace.

"God, you stink, and you look like crap," Jackie said.

"Well, I wanted to match the outside with the inside. Job accomplished," I said, kicking the door closed, watching Jackie make her way into my kitchen.

"Staci," she said, putting the ice cream in the freezer, "get dressed. It'll help you feel refreshed. Cleanse you of your sorrow." She walked into the living room and sat on the armrest by my head, dropping the coupon on my chest near the crusty Cheez Whiz smeared on my sleeve. "If we go shopping, you can't wear that."

"Why not? Wearing pajamas while running errands is the in thing now."

"Not ones that haven't been washed in days." Jackie pinched her nose.

"You're exaggerating. I don't smell." I rolled my eyes at her.

I sat up, grabbing my tea mug off the table. I took a sip then spat the cold liquid back into the cup.

"Yuck, this is from yesterday," I said as Jackie took it from me, pouring it down the sink. "I don't want to do anything today. I need to binge on Netflix with my best friend and forget about Greg."

"What exactly is the problem?" Jackie asked, hugging me from the side as she sat. She picked up the remote, turning off the flat screen television. "You're both columnists. I don't think you should stop him from sending pieces into your favorite magazine. Seems petty."

"I'm not petty. Greg lied. I gave him a chance to fess up, but he didn't take it. He told me he wasn't going to send anything in, but I already knew he got a job offer with the *New York Times*. How do I trust him after that? My career is the biggest thing in my life. I can't let it go, pretending I didn't see the e-mail."

"Did you ask him why he lied?"

"I didn't have to. I already know why. Greg is a smooth-talking, two-timing charmer who only looks after himself. I didn't have the energy to fight with him, so I just left. He knows how much I wanted the job at the *New York Times*. He even helped me prepare my proposal for them. Why would he do all that yet apply for a job behind my back? It's because he loves playing games. He wants revenge for my bad behavior toward him."

"That's a good conspiracy theory, but I don't think Greg has that kind of imagination."

Jackie turned off the television and turned to me. Placing her hand on my shoulder, she said, "You should talk to him. You keep making assumptions, but you don't know what his real intention was. Why are you really angry, Staci?"

"What?"

"Why are you angry? It's more than just Greg lying to you."

"He used me to get to my family to get his story. That's why he was asking all these questions, pretending to be my boyfriend. He was doing his research. I knew he had something up his sleeve."

"I don't believe you think any of it is true, right?"

I bit my lip before saying, "Okay, I'm jealous," I said, picking at the lint on my baggy shirt. "He surpasses me in so many ways, especially in our careers. They want guys like Greg at the *Times*, not me. I'm a B-rated choice. They'll never choose my pieces. Do you know how many times I've submitted to them?"

Jackie shook her head.

"Twenty-five over the course of two years. Every single one was rejected. Greg doesn't have to try, he gets a job offer thanks to his name. How is that fair?"

"Maybe you're trying too hard," she said softly, avoiding my gaze. "You want this so badly that your quality is affected. Don't forget, Greg has a couple of years more experience than you, but I've read your articles. I know you're improving every day. You need more time to figure out your specific style and find your voice."

"Whose side are you on?" I hopped off the couch and went to the freezer to take out the ice cream. Opening the top kitchen drawer, I pulled out the biggest mixing spoon I owned.

"I don't want to see you throw away a great thing with Greg because of a little misunderstanding."

I grabbed my phone off the counter, scrolling through my text messages while she lectured me on the work it takes to be in a relationship. *Please make it end!*

"Oh my God," I said, dropping my phone. My knees weakened, and I clutched my spoon.

"What is it?" Jackie raced to my side.

"I got a few texts from Kate. She said Greg's father is throwing him a huge celebration tomorrow at the office to send him off to his new position. They want to know what picture they should put on the cake."

Jackie gasped. "Why hasn't Greg told you any of this? Has he tried to call you?"

"Not once," I said, gritting my teeth. "Tomorrow, at work, Greg will be in for a rude awakening."

"Please don't revert to your old attitude, Staci."

"I'm not going to do anything drastic, except submit my resignation with Nast Publishing. That way, I never have to see Greg McAdams's face again."

"Love is a choice, and if you to love her not only today but here on after—then give it everything you've got."

How Do You Know It's Love?
by Greg McAdams

20

STACI

THE CHARITY EVENT Nast Publishing was hosting was tonight. Even though I had handed in my resignation, Kate had suggested I take two weeks off to think things over and begged me to attend this benefit. However, I didn't come for Nast Publishing or Greg. I came because I was part of the date auction that raised funds for the children's hospital, or else I'd rather be at home with a container of Häagen-Dazs, and bingeing on Netflix.

With Jackie's help, I went with the velour halter dress. I even bought a brand-new pair of stilettos with bows in the back, but not even they were making me happy tonight. I arrived at the party with Jackie and was relieved I haven't come face-to-face with Greg just yet— or maybe I have. Everyone is wearing a mask.

Nast Publishing had gone all out, renting the Great Hall at the Metropolitan Museum of Art. With its grand arches and marble floor, who would have thought the main entrance to the museum could also double as a ballroom? A live band playing jazz overpowered the murmurs of the four hundred guests attending tonight's event. But there weren't enough people to put space between Greg and me.

I was at the big hexagon reception desk, which now doubled as a bar, admiring the centerpiece, a big vase with wildflowers, when Greg stood beside me. He wore a plain black mask, but I would have recognized those eyes anywhere. He wore a black tux with a scarf that hung on each side of his lapel. He looked sharp.

"I missed you," he said, trying to grab my hands, but I dropped them to my sides.

"I'm too upset to talk to you right now." I faced the crowd, feeling his gaze burning into me.

"You don't have to talk, just listen. There's been a huge misunderstanding," Greg said, leaning forward. "I didn't take the job with the *New York Times*. I'll admit, for a short moment I did consider it because I wanted to prove to my dad that Nast Publishing wasn't my only option, that I didn't need his help. But I turned it down. I recommended you for the position instead, but I haven't heard back about that."

"You're just saying that to make me feel better."

"I'm telling the truth. I'm taking over Nast Publishing as CEO in the next few days. I know you're one of the best writers I've had the privilege of knowing, and you deserve a shot at a job at the *Times*."

"Why didn't you tell me anything?" I looked at him—his eyes were riddled with hurt.

"I wanted you to be surprised if you got the job offer. I talked you up so much; I thought they'd be begging to work with you."

"But hold on ... I saw the e-mail on Friday."

"Staci, that e-mail has been sitting in my inbox unread for months," he said.

I shook my head. "It doesn't matter now. I don't need you to come to my rescue."

I placed my order with the bartender in a black vest and white shirt, handing him a ten-dollar bill from my purse.

"I asked you to be honest with me, and you kept something this big to yourself," I continued, "You've lost my trust, Greg. Your ego is too big to be in a relationship with me."

"You know it's not true." he frowned.

I took my drink, ready to find Jackie, but Greg grabbed my arm.

"Don't talk like that. These last few months with you have been amazing. I wish you gave me another chance to make things right."

"No, I don't think I can." I glanced across the room, not able to look at Greg. I can't forgive him only for the fact he didn't try to reach out to me these last few days. If he knew I misunderstood the whole situation, why hadn't he show up at my apartment, forcing me to listen to him? "I gave Kate and your father my resignation. I was kidding myself to think I could ever be on the same level as the savvy columnist Greg McAdams."

"Staci," he said, "let me show you something. I worked on it all weekend. That's why I didn't call."

The nerve of him! Greg wanted to talk about work?

"We're done, Greg." I slipped out of his grasp and returned to Jackie.

When I plopped into my chair, my body felt like concrete. I didn't want to do anything except go home and sleep. Jackie looked me over, but I couldn't glance her way.

"Did you see the article Greg posted earlier on the magazine website?" she asked, picking my phone off the table.

"I probably saw it already. We both read the final copy before it's published."

Jackie pulled up an article page on my web browser. "You haven't seen this one, I can assure you."

"Jackie—"

Without another word, she placed my iPhone in front of me. "Read it. You'll have a change of heart."

I stared at *According to Staci & Greg*'s website and saw the title, "Open Letter to the One I Love."

"What is this?"

"Read," Jackie said, staring at my phone.

It's very rare when someone comes along and spins your world on its axis, and you have the kind of magic to do that. No woman has taken my breath away just at the sight of her like you have. And yet, despite our fallout, I've never questioned how you felt about me, and maybe I've never made it clear to you how much you meant to me. I should have run after you, but my pride got the best of me. So, here I am, telling you I am crazy, madly, deeply in love with you. And, ten years from now, I will think back to our time together and know you're the one who got away. I have no shame telling you that.

When I started writing this article, it wasn't meant to be for you. It was meant for people out there who were too blind to hold on to what they had in front of them, as I hoped they were not ignorant like me and making the mistakes I have. But it ends up, I wrote this for you.

So, thank you for the time we shared. I know I will love you forever and spend a lifetime trying to find someone like you to make me feel like that again...

I TURNED my head up toward Jackie, who was staring at me with hope.

"He posted this today?"

Jackie nodded.

"Before I turned him away?" I asked.

"I'm afraid so." Her lips thinned out.

I'd forgotten who I was. I'd grown so insecure with my past relationship, finding an excuse to leave before Greg could hurt me for real. I didn't have much experience with relationships in the past, and my feelings for him were overwhelmingly strong.

Suddenly, I felt Jackie's breath on my neck. I turned to find Jackie standing over my shoulder.

"He loves you, Staci," she said. "You see that, don't you? I know you're strong, but deep down, you still doubt your worthiness."

"Don't get all sappy," I groaned, flicking a tear from my eye. "I'm a mess. I blew it with Greg. It was nice of him to write it, so I guess it means we can part amicably."

Jackie sat down beside me. "Go to him."

"Jackie—"

"Go now!"

"I can fix things with Greg. I can tell him how I feel. Right?"

I looked at Jackie with doubt, and she nodded furiously.

"You're holding on too tightly to the past. Greg is not Luis," she said, turning me, pushing me to get up. "Go talk to Greg. Learn how to communicate with each other. Trust me—I'm married. I know this stuff."

Looking over my shoulder, I smiled. "I'll let you know how things go. Or you could come with me and help me swallow my pride? You've always been an amazing wing-woman..."

"Stop stalling— go!"

I heard Greg's name being called out, and my eyes divert to the stage in front of us.

"He's up there," I groaned, sitting back in my chair.

I completely forgot that Kate had signed Greg for the charity date auction, too. Greg did what he usually did; he flashed his charming smile and teased the crowd by unbuttoning his tux, opening one side of his jacket to allow the already-excited women in the room to get a glimpse of what they will get if they should win. *His rock-solid body.*

"All right, ladies and gentlemen, this is Greg McAdams. He's a journalist and a writer for *Avant-Garde magazine.* He loves motorcycles and long walks on the beach. His ideal date is experiencing new places and trying out new food. If he could travel anywhere, he'd go to South America," the announcer spoke into the microphone. "You're probably wondering what kind of date you can expect with New York's most eligible bachelor. Well, I'll give you two answers. One, you'll be riding on a motorcycle and holding on to his six-pack. And two, you'll have the best time of your life. Doesn't that sound exciting?"

The women in the room got rowdier, which caused me more grief. *I needed to stop this, but how?*

"Look at the way this kid is dressed—a real James Bond over here. Let's start the bid at one hundred dollars. One hundred in the front row." the announcer said.

"Hundred thirty." A woman in a pink mask yelled out, waving her arms in the air.

"Hundred forty." A woman in the far corner shouted.

"Hundred sixty." An attractive brunette in a skintight red dress waved her hand in the air.

"We've got a hundred sixty in the front." The announcer points. "Come on, ladies. You can do better than that. You get to hold on to Greg's pecs!"

"Two hundred."

"We've got two hundred from the woman in silver."

Things began to get serious when Greg pulled off his jacket and the women started whistling.

Animals.

"Three hundred," Jackie yells, lifting my hand in the air.

"What are you doing?" I whispered to Jackie.

"Doing you a favor! Are you going to allow miss voluptuous

thing over there to go on a date with Greg? No! So, get your butt off the chair and fight for your man." She yanks my arm and forces me to stand from my seat.

"Can we do two hundred and thirty?"

"Five hundred," the brunette in red who had a body like a cartoon yelled out.

My stomach twisted in knots.

Will she ever give up?

I'm *way* out of my budget— that was, if I had one before all this started. But now, I was in the thick of it, and I was in it to win.

"Six hundred," I called out, and my eyes met Greg.

From the look on his face, he was enjoying this.

"Seven hundred."

"One thousand," I chirped.

What was I doing?

"Can you afford that?" Jackie asked.

"Too late for that now, Jackie." I brushed the hair out of my face.

"Do I hear one thousand one hundred? Come on, ladies. Don't forget that it's for a good cause, and look at what you're getting," the announcer pointed to Greg as he removed his crisp white shirt and flipped it over his shoulder.

"Two thousand," the brunette in red called out.

Hell no, you won't, Jessica Rabbit!

"Three thousand!" My heart raced as I glanced down to see Jackie fanning herself. *God, I hope I have room left on my credit card. Do they even take credit cards? I freaking hoped so.*

Please stop bidding.

"Three thousand going once ... going twice ... sold! To the lady in black."

Damn, this will hurt, but whatever. I won!

"Go get him!" Jackie urged.

Holding my head high, I slowly walked toward the stage to Greg, who was now buttoning his shirt.

"Hi," I said, my voice cracked. "I read your article ... was it about me?" I said. I'd just spent three thousand dollars on a man, so I might as well cut to the chase.

"You're the only one I could have it written for," he said as he stared at me, making me feel like we were the only ones in the room—but we weren't. The silence only confirmed that we had a large audience watching us.

God, am I really on stage? I couldn't look at the crowd, instead keeping my focus on Greg.

"Is it true? What you wrote?"

"You know it is, or else you wouldn't be up here. You wouldn't have spent three thousand dollars ... when you know you already have me."

Three thousand? I don't even want to think about it.

"I meant every word, Staci," he said. "I hope I didn't embarrass you with it," he added, staring at me. "But I didn't know how else to get through to you, to make you understand how crazy I am about you. I don't want out—I want you."

My heart melted as I watched him cross the stage, making his way closer to me.

"I wish I could do something to express my feelings for you so publicly too." I smiled up at him, yearning to see his eyes.

"You can, just like this," he said, pulling me in.

Then, in front of four hundred guests, he kissed me as he'd never kissed me before, making me feel like I was his one and only.

EPILOGUE

STACI

A FEW DAYS LATER...

I WALKED to the room and opened the glass door of Greg's new office. I found him with his back to me, his hands in his pockets, staring out of the window. He had someone talking on the speakerphone, and it was business as usual at Nast Publishing. It hadn't taken long for Greg to fill his father's shoes. He was smart and creative ... and mine.

He turned to catch me staring. "Jack, I have to let you go. I have a beautiful woman in front of me I need to take care of. See you tonight at the Volary Bar."

"Hi," I said, closing all the blinds and shutting the door.

"What are you doing?" He chuckled.

"Fewer distractions."

"If you want to yell at me, can you do it some other time? I'm having trouble trying to figure out next month's issue. Our writers have several ideas, but none of them are aligning with the theme we want to achieve." Greg sat back in his chair, and I perched myself at the edge of his desk.

"I'm not here to yell." I laughed. "I caused much of the drama between us, huh?"

"Definitely."

I nudged him. "You weren't supposed to agree so quickly."

Greg leaned over and kissed my mouth. "Let's start over. I'll take you out for lunch, and we can pretend we're strangers again." He allowed his eyes to roam over me. Who knew what kind of thoughts he had in that head of his?

"I don't want to be strangers." I frowned, sliding off his desk and placing myself between his legs while holding his face with my hands. Now I had his full attention. "I want to keep things exactly how they are. You make me vulnerable, and that's not a bad thing."

"It isn't, as long as you understand I'm not going to hurt you, and I'll always be here when you need me,"

I stood, folded my hands, and paced around the desk. "I guess a small part of me felt ... as a writer, I was inferior to you."

Greg grabbed my hand as I passed, and he pulled me down again into his lap. "We're equals, Staci. I never saw you as anything else."

"I know that now. I was caught up in my head, constantly reminding myself of that chubby nineteen-year-old who had a crush on you. Sometimes, I thought you could see right through my charade. I've had an amazing time with you, but there was always a voice telling me that I didn't belong with you."

"You belong with me, never doubt that," he said and I felt the heat radiating off him. "But this would make a good theme for one of our magazine issues," he said, kissing my nose. "We could talk about men and women our age who still have insecurities that high school kids can relate to. We'll get video submissions of people telling their stories about mistakes in relationships and the deeper meanings behind their actions. Your story will be the first because women need to know who you are."

"My followers already know too much about me."

"They know the surface," he said, poking my chest. "But they don't know this part. The imperfections and the doubts. We can turn the past into your strength. Maybe then, *Times* magazine will truly see you, in your work."

"You really turned down a job for me?"

"Anything for you." His gaze locked on mine and my heart wanted to burst.

"I never had anyone sacrificing something that big for me."

"I meant every word I said in that article," Greg said, propping me up on the desk in front of him. He grabbed my hands and gently swung them. "I'm in love with you, Staci Cortés. I've never loved anyone as strongly as you."

I tried to remain serious, but a giggling smile broke out on my face. Pushing off his desk, I pulled Greg up, throwing my arms around him. Standing on my tiptoes, I brushed my lips against his ear. "I'm in love with you too, McAdams," I said in a low tone.

"Why are you whispering?"

"You didn't want me to yell at you."

"That I wouldn't mind hearing at full volume."

I threw my hands in the air and screamed, "I love your hot sexy body!"

Greg leaped towards me, covering my mouth, holding me close. "Keep your voice down," he hissed but couldn't hold back his laughter. "Do you really want people to hear that?"

"I don't care what they think."

"That's the Staci I know. I saw you let your walls down the first day I took you out on my motorcycle. You were finally acting like yourself."

"Because I was enjoying myself. Nothing was serious with us yet."

"Until now. Why don't we go out to dinner tonight, talk about where we're going to live?"

"What?"

"Well, my place is too small to house all of your shoes, and your place is ... let's just say, four is a crowd." His lips curved into a smile.

"You want to move in together?"

"I want more than that." Greg pushed his chair behind him with his foot and got down on one knee. He glanced up and grabbed my hands.

"What are you doing?" I frowned.

"What do you think? I'm trying to look up your skirt."

"Oh, stop it." I giggled until he pulled a velvet box out of his pocket.

"I know this might feel too soon, but I can't picture my life without you." His sparkling eyes met mine. "Will you do me the honor— be my one?"

I nodded my head as if I'd just come out of a daze. "I'll be your one and only ... forever." My eyes blurred as I leaned into a kiss.

"I need to call my family," I said, half in a daze. "My mother and grandmother will be so relieved." I giggled.

I can't believe this was happening.

"We should celebrate tonight with Jack and his new girl-friend at the Volary Bar," he said, kissing my neck. "Feeling up to it?"

"Sounds fun,"

"But first, I want to get you out of those clothes."

"What? Here?"

"Don't you think it will be more exciting?" he asked. "We'll have to be super quiet, which I know will be a challenge for you." He chuckled, and I slapped his shoulder.

"I'm so turned on right now," he said, backing me up, pushing his palms into the wall on either side of my head. "Can't wait to start our lives together,"

"Me too," I said, moving my lips closer to his.

Just then, Jackie barged in. "Oh, gosh! I'm sorry."

"Jackie!" I squealed. "What is it?"

"Mrs. Crawford is here, asking for you."

"From the *New York Times*?" I asked.

"Everyone in the office is talking about it. She's out front waiting to meet with you," Jackie said, out of breath.

I gasped and looked between Greg and Jackie, speechless.

"Greg, did you have something to do with this? Is she here because you asked her to come?"

"No, she's here because of your work and integrity. She wants to steal one of my best writers, and I will allow it to happen," he said, glancing down with loving eyes. "Go talk to her. I'll be here waiting."

I was excited and sad at the same time.

"What's the matter?" Greg asked.

"What about *According to Staci and Greg*?"

"There will always be *Staci and Greg*. This—what we have here, you in my arms—is all I need. As for the magazine, it will be called something else, written by someone else. Hopefully it will bring them much luck as it did with us." He smiled. "We've had a good run, haven't we? I'll miss working with you, but I don't want to get in the way of your dreams." He dropped his arms down. "Just go"—Greg kissed my forehead—"before I change my mind."

"I'll be right back." I leaped to the door leading to the hallway and then ran back to where Greg was sitting. I fell into his lap. "I love you, McAdams."

I kissed him one last time, and then I sauntered out of the room, giving him time to admire my figure before I went to set up a meeting that could potentially change my life.

AUTHOR'S NOTE

Thank you for taking the time to read my book! I hope you enjoyed reading it as much as I had writing it. Please take a moment to leave a review on Amazon for **The One & Only.** I would greatly appreciate it! Reviews help authors so much!

Hugs,
Maria

NEXT IN THE ONE LOVE SERIES

Want more of Jack Turner?

Cover coming soon!

Just One Look, coming May 2019.

What do a hotshot lawyer and a moonlighting beauty have in common? Not much, but when they have to put their differences aside for a good cause—anything can happen, maybe even love.

Add to Goodreads: http://bit.ly/2RpRiL8

The Proverbial Mr. Universe

Olivia Montiano is moving forward—without her unfaithful and controlling fiancé and without her father's unrealistic standards that have ruled her choices for twenty-three years. Olivia can now make her own decisions about life and love. But when mysterious, handwritten letters appear, she's baffled—and influenced by their very personal nature.

Nick Montgomery's life hasn't gone as expected. He's a washed-up artist and has decided that he doesn't need romance—until he meets Olivia. The universe then intervenes in their lives, making their paths cross again and again. But Nick is hiding something that he thinks could affect their relationship.

Will the universe bring Nick and Olivia together? Or will the mysterious letters and Nick's own secrets keep them apart?

CHAPTER 1

OLIVIA HAD FOUND an escape route on the far left, a red exit sign beckoning salvation but somehow she couldn't find the courage to venture out the door.

"Congratulations!" said an elderly woman, one Olivia didn't recognize.

"You look lovely. Are you having a good time, dear?"

"Thank you ... yes." She would have been, if the circumstances were different. If she weren't an absolute crazy mess.

Loud music and laughter circled around Olivia as she stood in the middle of the crowded room. Who were these people? They were too busy living their lavish lives to notice that hers was coming to an emotional standstill.

"Wow, some shindig you've got going on. I feel like I'm at the ... what's the name of that award show they do in Hollywood?" Paul asked, taking his place next to her.

"Are you talking about the Oscars?" She frowned.

And the Oscar goes to ... Olivia Montiano, for Sham of a Life. Too bad it had taken her five years to realize it.

Paul slightly nudged her arm, handing her a glass. "Are you all right?"

"Yeah, sure ... Why?"

"Well, you look a little pale." Paul playfully rested his hand on her forehead.

"Can you stop?" she laughed, slapping his hand away. "I'm fine."

Her brother Paul had always been handsome, tall and lean, but something was different about him these days. Maybe it was his light hair, freshly cut to a shorter length. Or maybe it was because he'd gotten his act together and now worked for their father.

"Yeah, I guess I'm a little overwhelmed." Olivia glanced down at her glass.

"Shit, do you even know these people?"

"Some," she said, smiling weakly. "It's overdone, right?" Olivia had had no part in any decision-making when it had come to planning her engagement party. Everything from the menu to the tablecloth was the work of Dario and the event planner.

"Well, your fiancé sure knows how to throw a party." Paul brought the glass to his lips but stopped midair. "Hey, isn't that the new mayor?"

Nodding, Olivia took a sip of her drink. "Geez, what is this?" She scrunched her nose.

"Whiskey." He chuckled. "Okay, drink up. It seems like you could use it."

Olivia wasn't much of a drinker—maybe a glass of red wine occasionally. Never in her life had she gotten drunk, because Dario thought it was immature. So Olivia had strived to be responsible ... maybe even a little boring.

Without hesitation she shot back the glass, wiping her mouth with the back of her hand.

"I didn't mean for you to chug it down. You're supposed to

sip it." Paul grinned, taking the monogrammed glass, with the initials *D&O*, from her hand.

She cast a glance over her shoulder and whispered. "Paul, do you have your cigarettes on you?"

"You don't smoke." His eyebrows gathered up.

"I'm an adult ... do you have one for me?"

"You're serious? I don't think it's a good idea."

"Come on. I feel like doing something destructive." Who was she kidding? She had never done anything bad in her life.

"I don't know what the big deal is. It's just a cigarette."

Paul peered around him, as if in deep thought. "All right, only this once."

"You're such a hypocrite."

"Do what I say, not what I do," he said, quoting their father.

Olivia rolled her eyes. "Where are you going?"

"I left them at coat check. I'll meet you outside in five."

She watched her brother make his way through the crowd. All night she had kept her composure: smiling, talking to her guests, even laughing at their not-so-funny jokes, never showing a clue about what was going on inside her. *Today is the day*, she told herself. She had reached the point of all she could bear. She needed to escape from this room, filled with people who believed social status and wealth were the only things that gave someone importance. At some point, she had been one of them, too.

Dario approached her from behind. "Olivia, come with me. I want you to meet Mr. Belanger."

"Who?"

"Come on. You know who he is." He cast her a look. "He owns half the commercial buildings downtown."

"Can it wait? I was—"

"Well, no. I don't want to keep him waiting." Catching his reflection in the glass window, he straightened his blue silk tie.

He gave her a side glance. "I told you, you should have worn the blue dress. At least we would have matched tonight."

Who were they, Laverne and Shirley?

"I don't believe this shit. I've been trying to close this deal for weeks."

Dario had been irritating her throughout the night. And now, she was less than excited at the prospect of being paraded around the room like she was the show's main attraction. Her fiancé seemed to have missed the point of what should have been a joyous occasion. Instead, he had made it out to be something else entirely. Olivia wondered how she had allowed herself to get lost in someone else's life. Was there any hope of getting her own back?

She nervously spun her ring around, itching to take it off like a cheap wool sweater. This ridiculous, massive diamond ring would have made most women happy.

Not her.

Dario hadn't proposed the way she'd dreamed of; instead he'd brought up the subject of marriage like it was a proposition for a business deal. She knew he wasn't much of a romantic, but still ... When they were ready to take the next step in their relationship, she'd never have thought it would feel like a hostile takeover.

He quickly glanced at her. "God, Olivia, would it hurt you to smile?"

She closed her eyes, held on to her last breath, and walked away.

"Olivia?"

Turning the corner, she opened a door leading to the large terrace. As soon as it closed, there was an instant quiet and serenity. Only the faint sounds of cars and trucks heading east and west came from below. The Place Ville-Marie had the most spectacular panoramic view of the entire metropolis, and this was the reason Dario had wanted to have their engagement at the penthouse. She let her long red dress drag through the snow, walking closer to the end of the gallery.

The beacon light flashed across the sky, forcing her eyes back up, landing on the biggest star. She had a feeling that something was about to happen, something exceptional.

What would she wish for? Happiness? Love? A great career? Didn't she possess those things already? Most of her friends thought so. But Olivia knew the reality: when it came down to the fine print, it was a different story. These days the thread had been unraveling quicker than she could ever have imagined.

For several weeks, Olivia had struggled with the feeling she was not living the life intended for her. Olivia thought about Dario. Even if she had believed in soul mates to begin with, it was clear that Dario wasn't hers. Over time, Olivia had thought she could change him, but it turned out it had been Olivia who had done the changing instead. At first she had told herself that Dario only wanted the best for her.

Lies.

She had thought she could live with the fact Dario was a workaholic, like her father, and it didn't bother her.

More lies.

She had believed Dario was marrying her because he loved her, and not because of her father's wealth or connections.

More. More. Lies.

The truth had been in front of her all along, but she'd refused to see it for many reasons.

"Olivia? What are you doing out here?"

She turned around and found her sister Nina standing there, with the door half open. Her purple dress fit Nina like a glove. Her honey-colored hair, pinned up, gave her the allure of old-Hollywood glamour. Nina was four years older, but everyone said they looked alike. Olivia had never thought they resembled each other much, except that they both had inherited the same big caramel eyes from their mother. Growing up they had been close; all three siblings had their place in the family: Nina was a daddy's girl, and Paul was a mama's boy...and Olivia fell somewhere in between.

"Geez, it's cold." Nina brought her arms up, bracing herself for the winter chill.

"Where's Paul?"

Nina shrugged. "He said you wanted to do something destructive. What's that about?" She paused. "Are you crying?" Nina pulled her dress up, carefully walking closer.

"I can't do this."

"What?" Nina frowned.

"I can't go through with this charade ... I can't marry Dario." She covered her face with her hands.

Nina yanked Olivia into an embrace. "Hey ... Hey, it will be all right. Liv, seriously, stop! You will get mascara all over yourself, and me." Nina pulled back and reached into her purse. "I know what's going on..."

"You do?" Olivia took the tissue out of her sister's hand, wishing Nina could just read her mind.

"It's just cold feet."

Olivia's heart slumped. She knew it was more than that, but how was Nina to know? Olivia had been hiding everything from her family. There was so much they didn't know about her relationship with Dario.

"I had cold feet before I married Peter. It's only normal. It happens to some people."

"I don't believe you. You're just saying that to make me feel better."

"No, it's true. Ask him." Nina's teeth chattered.

"But Peter is good to you."

"Yeah, Liv. All men are brilliant in the beginning. They bring you flowers, sweep you off your feet, and when you marry them it becomes a different story." Nina brought her arms higher around herself, bouncing back and forth. "Suddenly you become this freaking 1950s housewife. Picking up his dirty socks at the end of the bed. Every. Freaking. Morning. Somehow they seem to forget what the laundry basket is for." Nina pulled a face.

"But you love him."

"Sure I do. We've been together for so long, but sometimes I wish we could go back to the beginning." Her smile faded. "Marriage is not a fairy tale, Olivia. Other things come into the picture. Mortgage, bills, kids—life has a way of sucking the romance right out of it. There are days I swear Peter gets on my nerves. I could just choke him ... But when I force myself to stop and think back to the first moment I saw him, and why I love him, it renews my faith in us." Nina's eyes softened.

"I don't know..." Olivia understood that relationships went through all kinds of changes. They evolved into something else, leaving a remnant of their former obsessive, passionate love behind. But if you didn't have the love to sustain the relationship, any snag could cause everything to unravel. She had heard this speech or something like it before, from Aunt Teresa to the sweet Chinese lady next door. It seemed everyone had a piece of advice since she'd gotten engaged.

Her dilemma was simple: what if she was making a terrible mistake by settling down before meeting the person she was supposed to love? Even at the beginning of her relationship with Dario, she couldn't have called it a great love story. Olivia wasn't sure what had sustained their relationship all this time. Perhaps it was love, but lately she had realized it had been her father. He was the one who'd set them up.

There was nothing more motivating than the fear of disappointing a parent.

Nina jumped at the sound of a crackling noise behind them.

"Ma, you scared the shit out of me." Nina placed her hand on her chest.

"Girls, I didn't think you were crazy enough to be out here. Quick, get inside! You're going to catch pneumonia." Their mother's voice came through the open glass door. She looked sophisticated in her shift dress and white pearls, the Jackie O. look. Even though their mother had arrived in Canada as a young girl, she had never managed to lose her Italian accent when she spoke English.

"We're coming, Ma." Nina shook even more. "What the hell are you made out of? Aren't you cold? Please tell me you're ready to go in."

Olivia nodded.

"Are you okay?"

Olivia took in a deep breath. "Yeah ... sure ... I'm just overwhelmed."

She spotted Dario from across the room, standing close to a very attractive blonde.

At what point had she forgotten that there were other choices?

ALSO BY MARIA LA SERRA

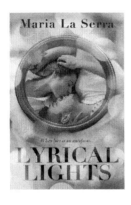

Lyrical Lights Mable Harper is a hardworking model trying to make her name in the fashion business. The only problem is that the world of fashion—and her agent—isn't really ready for a hard of hearing woman on a mission to challenge their patriarchal expectations. So after a string of unfortunate and unpleasant situations, Mable is relieved and glad her run of bad luck is over when a handsome, young stranger named Simon comes to her rescue at a bar. Then, when she runs into Simon once more before an unexpected opportunity revives her fashion career, she starts to wonder if it was more than a coincidence that she ran into this charming photographer.

As her modeling career flourishes so does her relationship with Simon —as he awakens desires she never imagined she had. However, as Mable falls more and more for Simon, she soon discovers there's more to him than wit and charm and his complicated past keeps coming between them.

Suddenly, Mable struggles to find a balance in her life in a world that keeps insisting on trying to tear her down, forcing her to choose between the life of fame that she always wanted and the man that, until now, she never knew she needed.

CHAPTER 1

MABLE

THE LITTLE ORANGE House was the latest trendy bar in the Meatpacking District, a hot spot for the arts and fashion crowd. With an unfinished degree in computer science, I was still trying to figure out where I fit into the fold.

The bar itself was chic, a mix of Spanish and industrial revival. To my left, there was a concrete wall lit up by candles, each in their individual compartments. All the way in the back, past the iron gates, was where I sat alone on a rust-colored leather couch, away from the crowd and the rhythmic music that played on the speakers. Rather, I assumed it was music, because everything sounded like ruckus. I rarely liked to come out to these places; the commotion and the background noise would annoy the average person, but it could be very stressful for someone hard of hearing, like me.

I had been waiting here for an hour, and it was clear that

Jason wasn't coming. But hey, I wanted to make it official. Besides, the martinis weren't half-bad.

Jason?

How can I explain my relationship with Jason? I guess you could say it was in eternal purgatory—it fell anywhere between hooking up and something of a real relationship. A girl can get lonely in a big city with no other prospects in sight. You take what you can get. Besides, I didn't have time for a real relationship.

That's a lie; time was what I had in spades. I was a broke model, working part-time at an Italian deli on the Upper East Side. Technically, I wasn't allowed to work anywhere while under contract with the NY Model Agency. They literally had me on standby, waiting for the next job, but I hadn't heard a peep from my agent in over three weeks, and my debts were on the rise. With what I got from my dad and what Johnny paid me under the table, I managed to survive. Working at the deli wasn't my dream job, but the owners treated me well, especially the little one they called Nonna. She heckled me every time I got in her line of sight. *"Eata, eata ... you too skinny.* Don'ta worry, you make the model anyway."

I was damn fond of them, but holy cow, what was with these people and their obsession with food?

I only wished my agent Dania had the same philosophy. The last time we had spoken, she'd said, "Darling, you need to lose three more inches, okay? Around your waist and thighs." The sound of paper crackling came through the phone—what I assumed was my contract compressing into a nice little ball—and I swallowed. "That's if you want to work. If you don't, it's not going to happen, not here in New York City or anywhere else."

She was oblivious to the fact that I was two layers deep in my lasagna.

"I'm sorry, Mable, but it's not working out ... I have to let you out of your contract." She'd sighed. "I wish you luck."

It was business; if she didn't make money, then I couldn't pay my bills, and, unfortunately, I was the product she was selling. We weren't having any success with each other.

But the worst of it hadn't come from Dania—it had come from the designers themselves, who had related their concern that I wouldn't be the best match to represent their label, since I was hard of hearing. It caused me to talk funny.

I asked myself, constantly, why the hell I put myself through this. It was straightforward: the dream was bigger than me. It was like an entity of its own, making me believe that, if I held on a little longer, if I could prove to them that my disability was an asset, I could represent girls who were different. I thought things would happen, just maybe.

So tonight, I had hoped Jason would be able to console me, like I had many times for him. I should have known better. When a guy said, "I'm not looking for a serious relationship," it most likely translated to, "I have no intentions of having one with you —like, ever." But my mind was a tricky little gal, the kind to concoct a better truth, one that suited me better. I had failed miserably at conforming him to boyfriend material, but I couldn't blame the guy. He had laid it out for me, but did I deserve better? Sure, I did. But I had allowed this shit-show to run its course for several months because I believed it was better than being alone. With every passing minute living in this metropolis, my views on dating had reformed into something more cynical. After a while, you realize that everyone around you complains about dating in New York.

As soon as I finished my glass, I ordered another one. I thought, *I surely deserve it*. I had a plan. Tomorrow I would call my dad and tell him he was right, that this whole modeling thing was a waste of time. In a few weeks, I would return home to

Montreal and continue my studies, like we'd agreed. But on the bright side, at least, after a year of putting my body through hell, I had been fortunate not to develop an eating disorder like some of my colleagues.

Within minutes, the waitress brought me an apple martini, and I reached over for my purse beside me. I swept my hand on the soft leather ... nothing. A surge of anger came over me.

"My purse was here just a minute ago, and now it's gone," I said, looking up at the twenty-something waitress, who looked like she couldn't be bothered. She repeated something, but I had no clue what Miss Muffet was saying. The music was blaring in the background, drowning the sound of her voice. All I could see was her bright pink lips flapping in the dark, but they were moving way too fast for me to catch anything. It's a misconception that a deaf or hard-of-hearing person can read lips—that we have developed a sixth sense to compensate for our disability. If that were true—I was still waiting for mine to kick in.

"Can you ask the bartender if anyone found a purple boho bag ... with a gold clip?" I was yelling at this point—I couldn't hear my own voice. She stood there, showing me my bill, and those damn lips still flapped.

"Yes, I would like to pay for my drinks, but someone took my purse ..." *This is crazy.* "I can't understand—I'm hard of hearing ... can you please write it on your phone?" I saw her smartphone peeking from the pocket of her black apron. Talk, talk, talk ... Her mouth kept going, and I was getting annoyed with her expressions. I was raised in the hearing world and had never deprived myself of anything any other twenty-one-year-old like me was doing. Never allowed my disability to impede anything.

Good grief, talk about an off night.

"Okay, just give me a second." Obviously I wasn't getting anywhere, and instead I focused on finding my bag. It was possible it could have fallen on the ground or gotten kicked under the couch. I got on all fours to look around, and that's when I stumbled across a pair of navy oxford shoes. I forced my eyes up the length of the muscular legs attached to them. Then a set of hands appeared, guiding me up, and I straightened my body.

When I did, my eyes met the most expressive, soft, ultramarine eyes I had ever seen. And I found myself speechless. I would have expected no one to come to my rescue, but there he was, with a laid-back vibe in his style. He'd come with a gorgeous smile and light tousled shoulder-length hair. Without a doubt, I knew I was in for some trouble.

"Are you all right?"

"Someone took my purse," I replied. I looked past him and realized Miss Muffet had disappeared.

"No worries. I took care of it." As he spoke, I looked at his face.

"Do you want to talk outside?" I pointed to my ear underneath my hair. He nodded, but I was aware he didn't grasp my situation. It was pointless to explain, but he would soon find out.

ABOUT THE AUTHOR

Maria La Serra lives in Montreal. Before becoming a writer, she worked as a fashion designer. She will try everything at least once, except for skiing, hiking or camping- okay anything relating to activities done in the great outdoors. When she's not working on her next book, you could find spending time with family.

Connect with Maria!

www.maria-laserra.com

authormarialaserra@gmail.com

Made in the USA
Columbia, SC
11 April 2019